Looking in the Shadows

Looking in the Shadows
The Life of Alice Austen

A Novel

Amy S. Khoudari

iUniverse, Inc.
New York Lincoln Shanghai

Looking in the Shadows
The Life of Alice Austen

iUniverse books may be ordered through booksellers or by contacting:

iUniverse
2021 Pine Lake Road, Suite 100
Lincoln, NE 68512
www.iuniverse.com
1-800-Authors (1-800-288-4677)

This is a work of fiction. All of the characters, names, incidents, organizations and dialogue in this novel are either the products of the author's imagination or are used fictitiously.

ISBN-13: 978-0-595-39165-3 (pbk)
ISBN-13: 978-0-595-83553-9 (ebk)
ISBN-10: 0-595-39165-6 (pbk)
ISBN-10: 0-595-83553-8 (ebk)

Printed in the United States of America

This book is dedicated to the memory of my mother, Gloria B. Silver. She always believed in me even when she disagreed with me.

Foreword

Alice Austen was a real person who was born on Staten Island in 1866 and died there in 1952. This book is a novel based on her life—a life that was distinguished by a talent for photography, but that was otherwise ordinary. By this I mean that, unlike many of her contemporaries, Alice Austen was not involved in the political and social reforms of the latter half of the nineteenth century. She was not a suffragist; she was not involved in the settlement movement or in the movement to remove corruption from government. She did not use her photography to document the plight of the poor. Austen was a very patriotic woman, who in the main seems to have been quite satisfied with the social status quo...and this is why I have chosen to write about her. We are so steeped in the history of extraordinary women that we tend to forget that most women lived their lives according to the social conventions of the day.

Why a novel? Alice Austen has left her record in her photographs, and it is a substantial record; the Staten Island Historical Society holds approximately three thousand negatives and twenty-nine minutes of home movies. In the 1970s, Ann Novotny researched Austen's life for a book of her photographs, *Alice's World: The Life and Photography of an American Original*. Novotny and her associates had the opportunity to interview people who had known Austen personally. The notes from these interviews and the book itself provided me with a great deal of biographical information. However, as I attempted to piece together a new biography of Austen, I realized that something was missing: Austen's inner life was not detailed in the written materials left by Novotny and is explained ambiguously at best in the photographic record.

What motivated Alice Austen to take the pictures she did? What went through her mind as she developed from a little girl living a life of privilege in America's upper class into an old lady who lived the last three decades of her life in increasing poverty? And all this happened before finally being discovered in the last year of her life. How did she come to terms with choosing to defy convention by not marrying? What were her feelings for Gertrude Tate, a woman she knew for fifty years, and with whom she lived for nearly three decades? We can only imagine. The clues are in her work, the Novotny interviews, and an apparently random collection of letters from friends that she saved, along with a scrapbook briefly kept, and some other odds and ends. But we need imagination to draw conclusions, and that is why this is a novel, not a biography.

This novel, then, is an account that presents my interpretation of Austen's inner life. I believe the slant of this fictional account has basis in fact. Most of the people in this book were or are real people, although I have changed some names. The correspondence in this book is based on letters from friends, from family, and from Alice Austen herself. It should be noted that Alice had many prejudices, and in this novel, wherever racial or ethnic stereotypes are mentioned, they reflect Alice's views as she expressed them in her correspondence. These sentiments are <u>not</u> my own. Alice's thoughts and the inner dialogue have been constructed by me alone but are based on conversations that she had in the last years of her life, her scant writings, and her thousands of photographs.

I know some will disagree with my perspectives on Austen's life, especially my theories regarding Austen's fifty-year love affair with Gertrude Tate, but they are my interpretations, and they are based on nearly ten years of extensive research on both Austen's life and the era in which she lived.

This book has been very difficult to write. I am a historian, and I am used to having previous scholarship and detailed sources to back up my conclusions. In a novel, none of that is required, so the assumption might be that this circumstance would be liberating for someone tied so closely to precedent and "fact." As I wrote this book, I felt as though I were standing on the edge of a precipice without a safety harness of previous scholarship, but I believed that if I did not take the chance of describing what I thought Austen's inner life might have been, I could not write her complete story. In order to get at what she was thinking, I needed to look beyond the obvious, just as photographic analysis is not simply a matter of looking at the light. In order to do Alice Austen justice, I needed to look in the shadows.

Chapter One

As I lie here, still and silent, staring at the bare lightbulb above my head, I wonder how I came to be here. How do I, an active woman who traveled, and who lived a wonderful and rich life, find myself gnarled by arthritis, confined to a bed, in this poor farm? They call this place the Old Farm Colony. Who do they think they are fooling? Everyone here on Staten Island, and probably everyone in all of New York City as well, knows that this is a place for the old, crippled, and destitute. I had it all, but now, if it weren't for my beloved angel Gertrude Tate's visits, I would have nothing. My family, save Gertrude, is gone now; my money is gone; and my home—my beautiful home—has been taken from me by those Italian newcomers, that immigrant family, who have no respect for its history and its beauty.

I know that it is 1950, but I am not sure of the month or the day of the week. Days and months have no meaning to me here; unless Gertrude comes to visit, every day is the same...except yesterday, when a man named Harold Oglesby came to see me, and he showed me glass plate negatives and photographs—my photographs. They were not my prints, but they were very large prints from my negatives. Trude was in the pictures, and Julia Martin, and Julie Bredt; Daisy and Carrie and Violet; even Henry Gilman, poor, sad Mr. Gilman—oh, how ardently he courted me. Mama and Grandfather were there, and it was as though my whole life began to play before my eyes. Where had I come from? Where had my life begun?

*   *   *   *

I would be remiss if I did not briefly detail my society's expectations of a lady of my standing. Growing up, I was taught that a lady always maintains a certain public image. Her public life must be above scrutiny to attract the best possible male suitors. A young lady's main concern is finding a fine husband, and her reputation is evaluated through her marriage. In reality the private lives of "ladies" did not reflect the public image. However, in this society, the image mattered more.

The beginning was simple and complicated at the same time. I was born on March 17, 1866, on Staten Island, at my mother's home, Woodbine Cottage. Actually the cottage belonged to my grandparents, John and Elizabeth Austen, who lived in their own home in nearby Rosebank. My grandmother called the Rosebank home "Clear Comfort." To us it was simply home. Even as a small child, I was struck by the astoundingly beautiful simplicity of my grandparents' home, with its grassy, well-tended terrace that stretched outward to New York City's Lower Bay.

My mother and I didn't stay at Woodbine Cottage longer than three years, and my father never lived with us, as far as I can remember. In fact I don't know anything about my father, other than his name, Edward Stopford Munn, and that he was English. He simply left one day and never came back; I never saw him. I was not allowed to ask any questions about him, and his name was never spoken. In fact my mother retook the Austen family name. That is how I, Elizabeth Alice Munn, became Elizabeth Alice Austen. I was never fond of the name Elizabeth (it seemed so old-fashioned), and when I was old enough to get my way, I insisted that everyone call me Alice. Of course that was confusing, since Alice Austen was my mother's name as well, so at home my family often called me Lollie, Lolla, or Loll, my childhood nickname. Everyone else called me Alice—Alice Austen. They never called me Alice Munn.

I must admit that as a child I was somewhat spoiled and got my way rather easily. I was, after all, the only child in a house full of adults, and I suppose that my grandparents and all the other adults in the house felt a little sorry for me because I had no father. Besides my grandparents and my mother, maids also occupied our home, along with my mother's brother, Uncle Pete (also known as Tim), who was only thirteen years older than me. He was more like a brother or a young, fun-loving father to me than an uncle. After I turned five, my mother's sister, Aunt Minn, and Aunt Minn's second husband—a rather distinguished sea captain, Oswald Müller—joined the household. Papa—that is my grandfather, not my father, of course—added an apartment to the second story of the house to accommodate them. We all called Aunt Minn and Uncle Oswald's apartment "the Quarterdeck," because they had their rooms done up like a captain's cabin on a ship.

Uncle Oswald and Aunt Minn were always fun, and I think that our friends and neighbors thought that they were, perhaps, unusual. They were known for being somewhat profane. In their bathroom, they had a collection of china figures on potties and in outhouses, which they called "the Potter Family," a not-too-subtle reference to Aunt Minn's friend Dr. H. Potter, the Episcopal bishop of New York. Aunt Minn and Uncle Oswald traveled to the Far East fairly often, and they always returned with unusual gifts: Oriental fans, large urns from ancient dynasties, and even a ginkgo tree, which they planted beside the house. I wonder whether those Italians who live there now have destroyed that wonderful tree. All of the rest is gone now; I know that the fans that hung on the walls of Uncle Oswald and Aunt Minn's upstairs apartment were sold off, and that the Oriental urns that graced the north slope of our terrace have been carted off by thieves or destroyed by vandals. The house is a mere shadow of its former self

June 21, 1869
Alice Austen Munn
Woodbine Cottage

Dearest Papa,

I have been thinking about your suggestion that Loll and I move in to Clear Comfort with you and Mamma. I realize that I resisted the idea when you first put it forward because moving in with one's parents after a marriage seems to suggest that one has failed. However, you are right about the difficulties of living alone, and it does seem clear that that horrid man who I married will never return to do what is right for his daughter and his wife.

Yesterday Loll and I went out for a stroll after our midday meal. I stopped into a shop and left Loll waiting by the door, as I was only to be a few minutes inside, and some neighborhood ruffians—little boys and girls about nine or ten years old—began to taunt my precious baby, saying that she had no father and implying that I had never been married! I whisked Loll home in tears (hers *and* mine, to be honest). Loll asked again about her father, but I would not tell her, except to say that he had gone home to

England. She asked again, and I told her sharply that was all that I was prepared to say on the subject. My poor baby girl looked so sad and so lonely at that moment, that I knew that I had to leave this lovely cottage in order to protect her feelings and encourage her happiness.

I know that you and Mama, and even young Pete, will do everything in your power to make Loll smile again. A young child needs a whole family, and I can think of no better family than my own.

Your loving daughter,
Alice Cornell Austen Munn

July 20, 1869
Alice Cornell Austen
c/o Clear Comfort
2 Pennsylvania Avenue
Rosebank, Staten Island

My dear Minn,

I do not know if my last letter reached you, as you seem to travel and move about so much, but I did want to make certain you knew that Loll and I have moved into Clear Comfort. Papa has gone to great lengths and great expense to make us comfortable. I love this home, and I adore sitting here on the piazza; looking across the terrace to the bay, I remember the happy times you and I had as children. Papa says that although he was reluctant to live here full time, he is happier in this place than he was in Manhattan. The air here is clear and healthy, and he says he knew he would not lose any children to epidemics on Staten Island, as he had on Manhattan Island. I know he and Mama miss our baby brothers who died in infancy, but Tim with his spirited nature and natural intelligence more than makes up for the loss. Did I tell you that Tim nearly blew the roof off the kitchen mucking about with his chemicals? Papa has been so patient with Tim's experiments, but he turned red in the face when Tim lit something explosive and scared the cats and the cook half to death.

Papa is so proud of all the improvements he has made to this tumbledown old seventeenth-century farmhouse over the last twenty-five years. He has designed a lovely, well-lit room on the ground floor for Loll and me. It is off the dining room and the middle parlor. There are large windows that look out on the piazza, so that in the warm months, we will benefit from the sea breezes off the bay. Papa has also considered adding a conservatory on the north side of our room, so that Loll can benefit from the sunshine and the "gardens," even in the cold winter months. I do think this will be a healthy and happy atmosphere for both Loll and me, and it will certainly be a change from the solitude and sadness of Woodbine Cottage.

Mama sends her love, as do Papa and Loll. We anxiously await your return.

Affectionately, your loving sister,
Alice Cornell Austen

P.S. Please notice, dear sister, that I no longer use that dreadful man's surname, Munn. What horrid sound! What was I thinking to marry such a ne'er-do-well?

Mr. Oglesby would like me to tell him all the details of my life. He tells me that his publishing house, American Pictorial Publishers, is very interested in publishing my pictures. But I think he has a curiosity about my story all his own. However, it all seems so long ago. My first memories are of being with Mama at Woodbine Cottage. We were so close then, and the recollection of her love for me is somehow reassuring, even at my advanced age. It was just the two of us at Woodbine Cottage—and the maid, of course. We would take afternoon walks, which were mostly pleasant, except when some young hoodlums would tease me about not having a father. Of course I *did* have a father; I just never saw him, and it was always clear to me that I was never supposed to speak of him—ever.

My first specific memory is of the moving day—that is, the day Mama and I moved out of Woodbine Cottage and into Clear Comfort. I imagine I had been there many times before, but the idea of living at Clear Comfort was so thrilling to my three-year-old mind that my first day at Clear Comfort left an indelible impression. Papa had purchased the home when it was a wreck—in 1844, I think. A Dutchman had originally built it as a farmhouse sometime in the late seventeenth century—1669, I believe.

Papa told me (not when I was three, but later, when I was older and interested in architecture) that the material used in the construction of the farmhouse did not stand up well in the climate of Staten Island. When Papa purchased the house and the surrounding property, the house itself was not suitable for habitation, and the grounds had returned to a wild state. Over the years, other owners had added several rooms to the original farmhouse—using the same unsuitable half-timber construction. So by the time Papa purchased the original structure, it had more than one room, but it was quite old-fashioned, in a state of extreme decay, and was too small for his growing family.

Papa's life had always been dedicated to making a proper home for his wife and children, so he decided to repair and restore the main parts of the house. He directed the builders to follow extensive plans drawn up by his friend, the famous architect James Renwick. Mr. Renwick (who had designed the new Grace Church on Tenth Street and Broadway in New York City) and Papa transformed the simple farmhouse into a comfortable summer cottage for himself, Grandmother, and the four children—Mama, Aunt Minn, and two boys who died in an epidemic in about 1850, when they were still quite tiny. Papa added several rooms to the house, along with a second story. The outkitchen was joined with the house itself, and Papa had shingles and wood siding added that were typical of the Carpenter Gothic style of architecture. In short he turned a humble dwelling into wonderful and comfortable home.

When Mama was about twelve years old, Papa decided the family should live at Clear Comfort year-round. Life in the city, while important for Papa's work, was simply not healthy for women and growing children. Papa had been truly devastated by the two little boys' deaths coming so quickly—both within a few months of one another, from typhoid fever.

I remember that going to live at Clear Comfort was like moving into a beautiful fairy tale. The broad expanse of the terrace reached out to the lower harbor. Incredible care was taken with the landscape. Papa often tended to details of the plants himself. I remember him standing on a ladder, carefully trimming the wisteria that entwined itself around the columns of the piazza. He would proudly point to the details of the house—dormers that he had added; the decorative cresting along the edge of the roof; the birdhouse finials; the chimney pots; the flair of the eaves; the beautiful, shaded piazzas; and the glassed-in conservatories off the parlor and off my bedroom. I loved the way the terrace crested at the stairs to the beach. The beautiful circular bench that Papa constructed under the tree at the top of the steps was a favorite spot for me, both as a child and as an adult. From there I could watch the sailing ships and steamships come and go. As a child, I would imagine I was an adventurer sailing on a boat to the far-flung and exotic places that Aunt Minn and Uncle Oswald told me about. As an adult, I spent many hours photographing the ships as they passed our terrace. I must have taken hundreds of photographs—I wonder if Mr. Oglesby has any of those plates.

∗   ∗   ∗   ∗

The next time Mr. Oglesby visits, it has been nearly a month since I've seen him. He asks me if I can remember when and how I began to photograph. I tell him that I remember; it is my body that is crippled, not my mind.

When I was quite small, Uncle Oswald brought home an eight-by-ten-inch glass-plate camera (which used a dry-plate gelatin process, not the wet-plate collodian process) from one of his trips; he was always generous. Uncle Oswald let me experiment with it when he left on another trip. I would say that is when I began taking photographs. I was quite young—perhaps ten, or maybe a little older...probably a little older, maybe fourteen. The dry-plate process was an extremely new and convenient advance of the old wet-plate process, which required that plates be sensitized immediately before exposure and processed immediately after. At any rate, by the time I was seventeen or eighteen, I was fairly proficient in the mechanics of photography and the preparing, sensitizing, developing, and printing of glass-plate negatives. My technique of lighting and composition was in its formative stages then, but it developed and changed over time, as did I.

From the beginning, Papa, Uncle Oswald, and Uncle Pete saw that I was very adept at working my uncle's bulky camera. In an effort to encourage me, Papa bought me my own camera, one that used four-by-five-inch plates. He and Uncle Pete got to work turning a large storage closet on the second floor of our home into a darkroom. It became my favorite retreat. It had been a large storage closet, but it became a very tight and tiny darkroom with no running water. I would often work late into the night, developing my negatives and working on my prints until I considered them perfect. Because my darkroom was dry, during the winter and summer, I had to wash the final prints at the pump beside the kitchen. I developed a system with a sort of water ramp that allowed me to pump the water while it washed over the prints in a continuous stream. I was such a clever girl with mechanics—not at all like the other girls. I remember being so impressed with my device that I photographed one of the maids engaged in that process. I liked to commemorate many of my ingenious techniques in pictures— often by tying my camera to a tree or perching it on several chairs, because a tri- pod was unavailable.

After 1917, when my grandparents and my mother were gone, Gertrude moved in with me. Our bedroom was right next to my darkroom. Gertrude teas- ingly complained about my rattling around with my trays and chemicals even after the mice had gone to bed. But we both knew I was a true amateur photogra- pher in the original sense of the word: I worked at photography for the love of it, and I devoted myself to my craft as if it were a lover. Gertrude was first in my heart, and my family was second, but photography was a close third.

I was always a perfectionist in the darkroom; Uncle Pete, who studied chemistry at Dartmouth and became a chemistry professor at Rutgers College in New Jersey, taught me the rudiments of mixing the developing liquids and the basics of developing the plates. Uncle Oswald showed me how to use the knobs and dials on the camera he brought home as a sort of lark, but for the most part, I learned by experimenting, so I was essentially self-taught. Unlike most of the girls with whom I was friendly, I was always mechanically inclined and loved to experiment with modern technology. I was an avid reader of *Popular Mechanics*, much to the dismay of my grandmother, who thought it strange that a young girl could be absorbed by materials that were usually only appropriate for boys. Nevertheless everyone in my household encouraged me in my pursuits, indulged me when I asked them to pose, and left me in peace when I worked endlessly in my darkroom.

Shortly after I began experimenting with Uncle Oswald's camera, George Eastman of the Kodak Company in Rochester, New York, developed a small, portable box camera. "You push the button and we do the rest" was the slogan for the camera. The idea behind the advertisements was that any woman could take pictures of her family and use the photographs to make an album that, like needlework, would enhance her home. The box camera Eastman created was very light and required no exposure adjustments. When the celluloid film in the camera had been exposed, the entire camera was mailed to Kodak, where the negatives were developed and prints were made. The whole package, including the camera—loaded with new film—was mailed back to the owner. All a girl had to do was mount her pictures in an album, or frame them and display them on the mantel in the parlor.

I was always one to experiment with new technological developments, particularly as they related to photography, so I acquired a Kodak push-button. It certainly was easy to use, but the quality of the images did not match the standards I had set for myself. In my estimation, nothing matched the results I achieved with the glass plates I developed and printed in my home darkroom. The process of exposing, developing, and printing with glass plates was time-consuming and required total accuracy. A small error in timing or in mixing chemicals could easily result in a ruined plate. Because photography with the glass-plate camera was so exacting, few girls felt competent to pursue it, even as a hobby. Not only was the equipment difficult to master, it was unbelievably cumbersome. My camera equipment weighed nearly fifty pounds and had to be transported in a wooden trunk. What normal girl could manage that? Needlework and painting seemed much more suited to the average feminine mind and body. But I was not an average girl.

*   *   *   *

My earliest photographs were far from adventuresome; I stayed on the terrace and photographed whatever was readily available, except people. I often spent hours on the circular bench under the tree. When I began taking pictures, I preferred stationary objects, because exposures were so long, and I was not yet familiar with all of the technical aspects of photography. I didn't want to inflict my lack of skill on human subjects, and I didn't want to subject the people I loved—my friends and family—to my fumbling with knobs and buttons as I familiarized myself with a new machine.

During our conversation, Mr. Oglesby seems fascinated with the fact that I have so many pictures of my home and the objects around it. I explain to him that I had loved our house and its gardens and wanted to commemorate them. This was true, but of course, another reason was that the house and its objects were available to me, and they did not move, so I was able to practice and become proficient with the camera. As I became better at making exposures and judging distances, I turned my attention to the boats that passed our terrace. I was always fascinated with sea travel and the idea of exotic destinations, so boats of all types were a favorite subject. Boats were my first *moving* subjects, and if I do say so myself, I was quite adept at capturing the changing scene from our terrace.

I worked diligently with the camera, so by the time I was twenty years old, I felt confident enough to take my camera around with me to various social events and even into the city, specifically for the purpose of taking pictures. I was always very careful to label the negative envelopes with the place, date, time, weather conditions, and exposures. From the questions Mr. Oglesby asks, I gather that at some point, the information had been somehow separated from the plates. How could someone be so careless with such valuable artifacts? I regret not taking more care of the plates myself. I can never forgive myself for holding onto them, rather than donating them to some museum or historical society. If it weren't for dear Lawrence Burton from the local historical society, who rescued them at the last moment, they would never have survived at all, I suppose. The man who bought the contents of my home told me at the very last moment that he would sell my precious plates for greenhouse glass. Imagine the gall of his planning to scrape off all the emulsion, as if my careful work were nothing. I wish I had made plans for my glass negatives and prints to be stored somewhere safe. It had always been my intention to donate my negatives to the historical society; I knew the pictures captured an era that had come to a close. I should have called Mr. Burton ahead of time. If I had, perhaps all the information I had written down so carefully would still be with the negative plates.

As a young girl, I had a scrapbook in which I pasted cards and invitations and news items of interest to me, but I never kept a journal the way other girls did. My photographs *were* my journal. I took note of where I went, what I saw, and what I thought with my pictures, just as other girls wrote in their diaries. There were letters, of course. I wrote and received many, many letters; sometimes I would commit a private thought to paper in my letters, but I no longer possess them. And that is a blessing; I would not be happy to have available for public scrutiny a written record of my trials and tribulations, small and large. To me the maintenance of privacy is a key virtue. My life, however, is recorded in my photographs.

*   *   *   *

Mr. Oglesby visits me again this morning to discuss his project. He explains how my photographs were discovered in a dank basement at the historical society, and that they were not organized in any particular way. Mr. Oglesby tells me something that I had already known in the back of my mind as I was taking pictures. He says that my photographs form an important historical record of New York and the country's past. He tells me he would like to publish the pictures in a magazine along with an article about my life. In order to do this, he says, he needs to visit me several times with pictures in hand to discuss what the photographs are of, when they were taken, who the subjects were, and what I was thinking about when I made some of my more humorous pictures. I readily agree, because he tells me there will be some money made from the sale of the pictures, and I am hoping it will be enough to free me from this wretched poor farm and allow me, perhaps, to be reunited with my Gertrude.

She's still the center of my thoughts. Even though she is partially blind because of her glaucoma, and her face is lined with wrinkles, she is a picture of ladylike perfection. No, it is more than that. Light does not merely shine on her face but seems to come from within. She walks as tall as the day I met her. Her hair is white and ever so soft, and her eyes are of palest blue. Even now there is a blossom in her cheek, just as there was on the day we first lay in each others' arms in the damp grass beside that Catskill stream. What she sees in an old crone like me, crippled from arthritis with bulging eyes and a bent-over shape, is beyond me. Yet Gertrude faithfully comes to visit me monthly. She feeds me and sings sweet songs in her angelic voice. And when she arrives or leaves, she kisses me sweetly on the lips. At those moments, I remember what it was to be young, tall, and energetic—running, sailing, bathing, playing tennis, and cycling. We are still so much in love that when I am with Gertrude, I feel like that thirty-one-year-old spinster who didn't have a care in the world. When she holds me in that last second before she leaves, I feel like the person she sees. I was never beautiful in my own eyes; I was always plump, and my eyes were overly large. But Gertrude thinks that both then and now, I am a picture of perfect womanhood.

Those sweet thoughts make me realize how difficult it will be to answer all of Mr. Oglesby's questions. He not only wants me to explain who is in the photographs and what the photographs are of; he would also like me to explain the significance of certain pictures. Remembering who and what the photographs are of will not be a problem; I have always been blessed with a good memory for detail. But when the pictures are of my friends and me at play, then it would be necessary for me to discuss some of my innermost feelings. This I cannot do. As a young child, I learned there is a large difference between a lady's proper public demeanor and what she might choose to do within the privacy and safety of her family's circle. There are certain things that a lady simply cannot do in public, and there are many things that she does not discuss.

In one sense, the rules concerning proper behavior for a lady were very confining at that time. It was important that a placid mood be maintained, and that women seemed restrained in their emotions. We compared ourselves with the working girls who, with their Old World traditions, were loud, effusive, and emotional. In their tawdry neighborhoods, they mixed freely with men on the streets and in bars; they were not only promiscuous, but they made love to one another on the streets for all of the world to see. A lady might walk arm in arm with another lady or her gentleman, but we would never consider hanging about one another's necks. Public displays of emotion—any emotion: joy, sorrow, anger, and passion of any type—were associated with slatterns and therefore were absolutely discouraged. Even as young children, girls learned that a moral, upright woman is one who acts like a lady at all times; making oneself presentable, performing one's duty, and making a proper appearance at social events is more important than one's own selfish needs. This was true for me and all my friends, and I am sure that the lower classes believed that the restrained demeanor we all displayed in public carried over to our homes as well. I am sure they envisioned our private lives to be as cold and reserved as our public lives.

To some extent, we were restrained in private, carefully choosing with whom we would be ourselves and with whom we would talk about the emotions that were forbidden to us in public. I was never terribly open with Mama or my grandparents. But I sometimes shared my feelings with Aunt Minn. She was the member of our household who would understand. She and Uncle Oswald were adventurous and perhaps a little wild themselves. When I looked at Mama, it never seemed to me that she had been young, because she was always so quiet and somewhat sad. But Aunt Minn was different. She was full of smiles and told jokes that shocked everyone in the house but me. She was not above raising her skirt above her ankles and doing a jig. When I was unhappy or confused, I could talk with Aunt Minn. Mama was always there with comforting words, but Aunt Minn seemed more able to understand the basis of my bad moods. But even Aunt Minn never would have understood the depth of my crushes on girls, so those I kept mostly to myself when I was around my family.

Our home was generally a place of comfort and calm, but we are human after all, and have human desires and emotions: so when I was alone with my closest friends—Trude Eccleston, Julia Martin, the Ward sisters (Carrie and Violet), Julie Bredt, and Daisy Elliott—I felt more free to express myself as I wished. I often used my photography to work out certain sentiments: my thoughts about courtship and marriage, my high regard for women's abilities, and my crushes on and attractions to other girls. My pictures helped me sort out my changing sentiments regarding who I was and how I wanted to live my life. I had a sense as I grew older that while I could love other girls intensely, I could never feel that way about any gentleman. This is just the sort of thing that I do not feel I could discuss with Mr. Oglesby, because it is simply not the sort of thing a lady should discuss with someone outside of her circle of close friends.

But Mr. Oglesby seems to want to know everything about my life. And it is all there; it is all in the photographs. There's nothing from my early childhood, of course; even later, not *all* of my life is clear to the eye of an outsider. But my coming of age is there, if you know where and how to look. I don't believe that everything is obvious, but it is there; I often created *tableaux vivants* of a humorous nature to express my true sentiments. So the question I must answer now is, "How much should a lady tell?" It will be a simple matter for me to talk about photographs that are less personal in nature. The truth is, however, that many of my pictures are deliberately obscure in order to keep my inner life hidden. And I do not wish to reveal myself now, even for the sake of making some much-needed money.

Given the nature of my upbringing, some of my circle considered some of my more personal photography to be a curious activity. Photography has such a public quality about it; it is most often displayed on one's mantel or used to illustrate and memorialize an event. I cannot say what exactly drove me to explore my innermost feelings in this medium, but I do know that I felt a compelling need to do so. It's unfortunate that my private outlet is such a typically public forum, but photography is the best form of expression for me.

When I reached a marriageable age and felt resistant to the idea of marriage, I was troubled. By exploring the idea that my attractions to women were more intense than those I had to gentlemen, I felt I was beginning to come into contact with something deep within myself; I felt more alive than ever before. Actually I felt absolutely free. And this freedom allowed me to reach out to other girls who had intense feelings for other women, searching for my own true love: Gertrude, of course.

I enjoyed making the pictures that dealt with my growing sense of self, but even as I made them, I knew I could never display them publicly. I was subtle as I could be and used humor as a tool quite often. But I am a lady, and if I displayed all my pictures and talked about their secret meanings, it would be the same as opening my diary to the entire outside world. Never in my wildest imagination would I have ever considered publishing all of my pictures, and even now, all these years later, I know that to discuss them with Mr. Oglesby would be a violation of my most firmly held convictions.

But I would so like to be free from this place and be reunited with my Gertrude.

Chapter Two

I must have fallen asleep last night thinking about my beautiful home, because for the first time in a long time, I had a lovely dream about Clear Comfort. My dreams recently about my home of seventy years have not always been pleasant. I am still confused about how I came to be dispossessed just after the Second World War. Papa died in 1894 and left the house to Uncle Oswald, who in turn left it to Aunt Minn and me when he died (Mama and Grandmother had already passed on). So when Aunt Minn died, the house became Gertrude's and mine.

My beautiful Gertrude moved in with me in 1917. I cannot believe that I knew and loved that lady for twenty years before she consented to move in with me. As long as I can remember, there had always been a sufficient amount of money to pay the expenses…but then, somehow, when the stock market crashed in 1929, the funds that had always been there dried up. I suspect that a cousin of mine, Harry Winthrop, absconded with my money, but he claimed that my loss was the result of investments that went under.

Even as our funds dwindled, Gertrude and I had wanted to continue to take in the cultural life of New York, to summer in country or at the shore, and to tour the great cities of Europe, as we had done many times before the Great War and the crash in 1929. To maintain our lifestyle, I went to the bank, and they allowed me to borrow money against the house. I did not think paying the money back would be a problem, but it became one. Gertrude and I struggled mightily. Because ladies were not taught how to manage finances, we never quite knew what to do. What do ladies of my standing know about handling money?

We started a tearoom at a small cottage in the neighborhood for which we paid a small rent. But later, when the expense of the rent became too much, we established one at Clear Comfort itself. Still, Gertrude and I always had trouble setting prices in order to turn a profit, and finally the tearoom was ordered closed during the war, because our property offered a strategic view of New York Harbor. The government inspectors were nervous about the possibility of German spies taking inventory of American shipping as they dined at our tearoom on my Gertrude's special lobster Newburg (a recipe that Gertrude acquired from the chef at Delmonico's, a favorite restaurant of ours and of all New York's elite). One time a spy was actually arrested on the property. It was all terribly exciting that day.

The tearooms—the first one at the cottage and the second one on our terrace—were quite a bit of work for us, because Gertrude and I were both getting on in years. I was not accustomed to working; girls of my class were not expected to engage in paid employment. But we did so enjoy running our little establishments. It was nice to have people come by and dine on small, elegant meals. It provided conversation and a break from the day-to-day routines that were somewhat dreary after the stock market crashed. Unfortunately the tearooms never provided the necessary income to pay back the loan and our expenses on the house, and then, when the government shut us down…well, that was the end. As Gertrude and I continued to struggle financially, I would occasionally sell pieces of jewelry, artwork, or some of Aunt Minn's Oriental treasures. I sold tea sets, furniture, and some china to raise money.

During the Second World War, Gertrude and I took in a tenant, renting an apartment on the second floor of the house—Aunt Minn and Uncle Oswald's rooms, actually—to a navy doctor and his wife. They were lovely company, and they loved to hear Gertrude and me talk about our lives before the stock market crash—we lived like *ladies* then, going to the opera, dining at wonderful restaurants, and wearing beautiful custom-made dresses, along with hats and white gloves. All of our clothes were custom-made, many of them on our trips to Paris.

I wanted nothing but the best for Gertrude and myself. We were ladies, and we always dressed and acted the role exquisitely, even after our finances tightened. It galled me that we had to wear mended clothing that looked shabby. In my youth, I never went for frilly fashions, but my clothes were always of the latest style.

The house fell into disrepair, despite our best efforts. Even the kindness of the bank officers who permitted us to pay only $10 per month to remain in the house after we were unable to make the actual payments was not enough. Gertrude and I had to maintain the house ourselves. As we had no money to replace things such as the boiler and the roof, the house became as shabby as our wardrobe. The house was quite run-down. With nowhere else to turn, and in desperate straits, I did what was necessary, in spite of my breeding. I begged money from my stingy, preachy cousin Harry Rogers Winthrop, who gave me a miserly monthly allowance of $25, which he quite grudgingly raised to $50 when it became clear that the lesser amount would not suffice. The greater amount was insufficient as well, but as I was a beggar in my own family, I had to be satisfied with what the "gentleman" gave.

Alice Austen
2 Pennsylvania Avenue
Rosebank
December 30, 1940

My dear Harry,

How can I thank you enough for your timely help that enables me to pay installments on my electric light and telephone bills—and even to buy some oil for the oil burner? These bills worry me constantly, as I have nothing to meet them with unless I can sell some of the Oriental china or other items in the house, which is very difficult to do in these times. My arthritis prevents me from walking far, and with no car, I cannot even consider selling the preserves that my friend, Miss Gertrude A. Tate, has made, or any of the other odds and ends from the house. People promise to come by to see them, but they do not. I dread the harsh winters! There was no heat in the house during the cold days, because I could not pay for oil, and the cold makes me very stiff.

My friend, Miss Tate, who lives with me under these trying circumstances, teaches dancing, but the classes are very small this year, and what she earns does not last long.

To try to save oil, I have closed up half the house, as you suggested. I will try to find out if Grace Church gives any help, but I do not go there regularly. You see, things are very desperate. I feel that I ought not bother you, but I have no one to turn to, and you have been so kind thus far. I am hoping that perhaps you may hear of some aid society—old age and poverty are very hard to cope with, but I keep trying and am thankful I am allowed to stay in my dear home. I am very sorry that you are not well, but you are under a heavy strain in these unsettled times and must take care of yourself. Thank you from the very bottom of my heart, and I'm hoping the New Year will bring you luck and happiness.

Most sincerely, your cousin,
Alice Austen

P.S. Forgive this long letter, but I wanted you to understand the facts, and that I would not ask for help without being in great straits. My writing is very bad due to the arthritis in my hands. AA

Alice Austen
2 Pennsylvania Avenue
Rosebank
May 15, 1941

My dear Harry,

Although I have tried very hard not to bother you again, I am forced to beg of you to help me, if possible—I literally have not a penny, but owe to the grocers for simple food. There is no profit from the tearoom, but a trifle comes in now and then. I am thankful to be able to stay in the house, as I have not a cent to board anywhere if driven out. The situation is terrible, and I do not know what to do. I would work at anything if I could, but arthritis handicaps me, so I cannot walk far. Miss Tate's dance classes were small during the winter term and did not meet our needs, even though Miss Tate used all she had to keep us going. I am trying to sell things, but buyers are few.

I trust that you will understand how hard it is for me to write this and how much I appreciate all you have done for me in the past.

Your affectionate cousin,
Alice Austen

Gertrude A. Tate
2 Pennsylvania Avenue
Rosebank
May 22, 1941

Dear Mr. Winthrop,

Thank you for the check for $50 that you generously sent to your cousin Alice. I am writing to let you know that the monies will be used to enable us to stay in our home, and for this we are eternally grateful.

With sincerest regards,
Gertrude A. Tate

Alice Austen
2 Pennsylvania Avenue
Rosebank
November 13, 1941

My dear Harry,

I feel very reluctant to bother you with my troubles. I have been meaning to write to you for some time, as I often think of you. I trust that in spite of everything, your health has improved. My situation at present is quite desperate. About three weeks ago, my oil burner gave out, and the serviceman who put it in twelve years ago says that we must replace it with a new burner. A new one will cost $200, and a reconditioned one will cost $125. We have had no heat in the house for a month, and the frigid cold is making my arthritis very stiff and painful. The Edison Company demands a minimum payment of $25 on my $45 bill.

The telephone company also wishes an immediate installment, and the local tradespeople have received no payment for over a month. The bank that holds the mortgage refuses to make repairs; they just tell me to vacate, so they can pull the house down. I have been paying them a nominal rent of $10 per month and am taking good care of everything. This house was built before 1669; it is the oldest on Staten Island and should be preserved. My cloth coat and my old fur hat are in storage, and I cannot afford to pay to take them out. There is an old-fashioned range in the kitchen, but it must have coal. There is a wood-burning fireplace in the parlor, but there is no one to cut the wood. I applied for an old-age pension, but they insist on knowing what I had twenty to thirty years ago, where it came from, and what it was spent for, along with who my brokers were, and so on. My brokers have long since gone out of business.

My only wish is to stay here for a few more years; as I am seventy-five, they cannot be many more. Can you help me a little over this dreadful situation? You have been so kind that I cannot bear to ask again, but I do not know what to do. I am sorry this is so long, but I feel that I should tell you all.

Your unfortunate, but affectionate cousin,
Alice Austen

Alice Austen
2 Pennsylvania Avenue
Rosebank
May 20, 1945

My dear cousin Harry,

The bank has sold the house over my head without notice of any kind to an Italian saloon keeper; he has put it in his daughter's name, and she is putting us out as soon as possible. The four portraits that you took in exchange for the money you were kind enough to send me are still here. Shall I send them to you? I have not been able to find any place to live, as apartments are scarce due to the war. Miss Tate is with me, and we are in despair. Things will have to be sold—a crafty Jew from New Jersey named Jaffee has agreed to buy the contents of the house for $600. This should enable us to move and pay the earliest installments on the rent. There is a tremendous demand for housing, and everything is so expensive that I do not know what we shall do when that money runs out. Our distress seems to be endless, and our situation is desperate.

I shall miss my house more than I can tell you, but my financial situation is so serious, there are no other choices. The house itself is in disarray. The hurricane last September caused a tree to crash across the wires near the kitchen, so the electric company cut off our electricity. We had no heat or light for over two months. The water pipes froze and burst the radiators, and we have had no cut wood for a fire since January. I am lame and have to walk with two canes, and there is so much to do to prepare for our move. It is a frightful prospect. I am sorry to have to write you such a woeful letter in pencil, but even my pen has broken down, and I cannot afford to replace it. I trust that your health is good and regret that I have to write of such miserable conditions here.

Your affectionate cousin,
Alice Austen

*   *   *   *

I hated to beg for money, but keeping Clear Comfort was so important. In the end, the bank officers who had been so kind to us moved on, and the new officers withdrew the agreement that I had had with the old bankers, refusing to accept the $10 per month rent. In 1944 they foreclosed on my home. We were able to stay on through the end of the Second World War thanks to the Office of Price Administration, which ruled that since the new owners of the house planned to open a restaurant, we could not be put out of our home. During the war, residential space was at such a premium that the rule was that no one could be forced out of his or her home for commercial reasons. But with the end of the war in 1945, Gertrude and I were forced to leave.

We took an apartment nearby, and we moved everything we could. The Mandias, an Italian immigrant family who owned a seedy bar on New York Avenue, moved into my home with the intention of setting up a new restaurant on our property. I have heard they were unsuccessful. What did those bar-owning immigrants know about setting up a restaurant in so elegant a setting?

Gertrude and I moved everything we could into our new apartment, and what we couldn't move we sold to that Jewish man from New Jersey. He certainly lived up to the reputation that Oriental Jews have for milking the old and sick of every penny and nickel that they can. I remember being told as a child that a successful Jew was a man who owned a pawn shop. And Mr. Jaffee was no different. He arrived on the appointed day, and he began to remove every item in our home. As I followed him about, I would see a memento here or a small object there that I wished to keep, and he would engage me in a tug-of-war over them. He claimed that the $600 he had agreed to pay us entitled him to the complete contents of the home. I begged him to let me keep a few things, and in the end, he took pity on me. I was quite hysterical, and our friend Mr. McMillan came over to help us gather what we could.

Actually we managed to salvage quite a bit, and our apartment, which was considerably smaller than our home had been, was filled to overflowing with precious pieces of furniture and knickknacks that my family had collected over the generations. It was difficult to move about, and the few friends who came to visit continually told us that we should part with some of these things. But my family, save Gertrude, was all gone, and this was all I had of my wonderful heritage. How could I let anything go? Having to move from my family's home was heart-wrenching enough.

Our stay in that apartment was short-lived. As I had told my cousin Harry, I had no money for rent, and we could barely scrounge enough for food. Finally age, poverty, and illness got the best of us. I was becoming increasingly crippled by arthritis, and Gertrude was beginning to lose her eyesight. We had to face reality, however harsh: we simply could not go on living together in that apartment. After thirty years of living together, Gertrude and I were forced to separate. I moved to the first of several horrible nursing homes—these ignorant nurses simply didn't know how to treat a lady—and Gertrude moved in with her sister Winifred and Winifred's husband in Queens, ever so far away.

I had no money for private residences, and the nursing homes were unlivable anyway, so I took an oath of poverty and committed myself to this dreary poor farm, where each and every day is the same, unless my devoted Gertrude is here on one of her monthly visits. Most of the time, I am resigned to spending my days here, in a ward with mostly silent, sometimes moaning, old women. But when I think back, I am so sad…perhaps it is best not to think.

Chapter Three

I must remember to tell that Mr. Oglesby when he comes again about my lovely, beautiful Gertrude. What a wonder she is! As frail and delicate as ever, but now partially blind, she travels all the way from her sister's home in Queens to visit me here in this sorrowful place. She is really my only regular visitor, aside from that nosy little secretary of my cousin's, Miss Whatever-her-name-is, who comes now and again. I suppose she is trying to be kind, but it feels as though she comes to visit so that she can report back to Cousin Harry about my "dreadful" circumstances. But Gertrude's visits are a joy. It is hard for me to believe I ever lived a life before I met the lovely Miss Tate. My meeting with Gertrude was fortuitous, and I have always believed that fate played a hand—a wondrous hand.

It happened in the summer of 1897—a time in my life when I was as certain as anyone could be that I would never marry. My friends and family, however, encouraged me to continue looking for a suitable gentleman, and since summer was a prime season for socializing with eligible bachelors of all ages and stripes, these same people urged me to travel to the summer resorts in upstate New York. The mountains seemed to attract everyone at that time of year. The city streets, of course, were terribly hot and crowded, and the bad air seemed to waft across the bay to our doorstep. At the very least, a month in the mountains of New York or Vermont offered me a respite in the form of cool lakes for bathing and sailing, shady trails for hikes along cooling streams, and opportunities to play tennis. The soft summer breezes of healthy air put roses into a girl's cheeks.

As I well remember it, in August of 1897, I left Clear Comfort for several weeks, traveling this time to visit my childhood friend Trude Eccleston, who was summering with her husband, Mr. Barton, at her family's vacation home at Twilight Rest in Catskill, New York. I didn't often vacation with my own family, because Mama was reluctant to travel at all, so she stayed at home for the entire summer. As a child, I would often go to Lake Mohonk with Papa and Grandmother, but I had tired of being with the older set by the time I was fourteen. Some summers I would visit Uncle Pete, who, after he married Nellie Munroe, moved to New Brunswick, New Jersey. Other summers I traveled to the mountains to visit various friends, like Julia Martin or my cousin Emmie Van Renselaer at her home in Fishkill, New York, Presqu'ile. I certainly enjoyed visiting with the Ecclestons, and I knew that Twilight Rest would be a tonic, because it was such a beautiful resort. No one could actually own the cottages at the Rest, but families like the Ecclestons held ninety-nine-year leases on them. So spending the summer at the Ecclestons' in the Catskills was like coming home. Even though Trude had married, she continued to invite me to her family's cottage—hoping, I suppose, that I might finally marry as well.

It seemed that Trude and I had been close friends since the beginning of our lives. Her father was the rector of our church, St. John's Episcopal on Staten Island; that is how I first came to know Trude. Over the years, we had so many adventures together, and I often felt she was the sister I never had. For the longest time, Trude and I shared almost everything; we seemed so close at times, it was as if we shared a soul. I remember one photograph that I took one summer of Trude and me wearing masks in our slips, with our hair down. We held cigarettes (but we didn't smoke them), and we posed as mirror images of one another, as though we were one.

Trude Eccleston Barton
Twilight Rest
Catskill, New York
18 July 1897

Dear Alice,

Our family is having such a lovely summer at Twilight Rest this year, and all seems especially perfect, except that your absence is felt deeply by all of us. The girls are friendly, and we have taken several walks along the trails that you love so. The gentlemen are interesting as well, and several who already know you are anxiously anticipating your visit. Will you be arriving soon? Do not forget to bring your camera; we might fail to recognize you if you did not arrive with that weighty trunk. There are several new people here this summer, and I think it should be fun for you. I am sorry that this note is so brief, but I must close, as I wish to put this letter in today's post. Please send my love to your mother and especially to Mrs. Müller.

Your most affectionate friend,
Trude

*   *   *   *

So in the summer of 1897, Trude invited me to visit her at her family's summer cottage. I packed my trunks—one for clothes and a separate one for cameras, chemicals, and plates—and off I went. Trude had been married for a number of years by then and had three beautiful boys. I was thirty-one years old and still unmarried, so although I still loved Trude, we did not have as much in common as when we were girls. Not that I hadn't had my suitors—I told myself and others who asked that I simply hadn't found a gentleman that was good enough for me—one who could match my athletic abilities and my talent for photography. If I was an old maid, then I was, by golly, an old maid by choice! At that time, I thought that perhaps I was married to photography and had no time to be a proper wife—and no real desire to be one either, I might add.

From the time I was sixteen years old, I received invitations to dinners, balls, and parties, and I was encouraged to attend them. It was just the natural course of things that once a girl was four years shy of twenty, her social life would be conducted with an eye toward meeting a gentleman who would make a suitable husband. All of my friends at that time, who were my age, were anxious to make sure they did not become spinsters. By the time I was eighteen years old, most of my friends were engaged…but not I. All of the girls with whom I had grown up were anxious for me to attach myself to a particular young man, and so almost all of my correspondence with them dealt with their meeting their future husbands, all of whom seemed to have friends that they would like me to meet. And while I did enjoy the social whirl, and I did like some of the boys, I did not find myself attracted to the gentlemen in the way that many of the other girls were. To me none of the men were suitable partners. In fact I could never imagine being attached to the boys in the way I felt attached to the girls in my set. I felt so passionate about girls like Trude—in fact I was somewhat distressed when the girls began to marry and leave me behind. This was not because I wished to marry like them; it was because I loved them so. And I think, looking back, that I was truly in love with Trude, and she loved me—but not in that way.

The boys did seem to like me, though. I remember in particular the summer that I was twenty-two, everyone thought I would become engaged to Mr. Braddish Carroll, and I think that Mr. Carroll did believe I would one day marry him. I would often see him at dinners, and more importantly to me, he liked to play tennis and often competed in tournaments.

December 3, 1888
Mr. Braddish Carroll
New Brighton, Staten Island

My dear Miss Austen,

I have to thank you very much indeed for giving me one of those prints of the tennis match, as I particularly wanted it. I found it at home when I got down from the city today. Had I known it was on the way this morning when I met you on the boat to the city, I most certainly would have thanked you in person.

I am going to frame all of them and hang them in my room so as to keep two pleasant days fresh in my mind. Hoping to have the good fortune to meet you soon at some of the dances. Believe me.

Most sincerely yours,
Braddish Carroll

*   *   *   *

I think that the fact that I took many pictures of Mr. Carroll led him to believe that I liked him much more than I actually did. While he was falling in love with me, I did not feel the same. I liked him quite a bit, but simply as a friend and tennis partner, not as a future mate. The same thing happened with Mr. Will Batchelder, whom I met one summer at Twilight Rest.

December 22, 1889
Mr. Will V. Batchelder
New York City

Thank you for the photographs, Miss Austen. They are so beautifully taken and are a pleasant reminder of our week together in the mountains. Notwithstanding the "spell" under which I labored at that time as we walked beneath the cover of the trees beside the rushing streams and crashing waterfalls, there were several days that were pleasant ones to me and in spite of the fact that I have foresworn such spells in the future, I am confident that every time I am in your presence, I will fall under a spell. Nevertheless I hope that you will find me more companionable should another such outing throw me in your society, which I sincerely hope will be the case.

With wishes for a cheerful Christmas and a Happy New Year to you and your family. I am most sincerely yours,
Will Batchelder

February 1, 1889
Will Batchelder
New York City

My dear Alice,

I have just written a long letter to Miss Eccleston trying to make my peace with her and am impelled to scribble first a few lines to you to the effect that though lost to sight, as it were, you are still clear in my memory, and I sue for forgiveness for my apparent neglect.

My father has had his eyes operated for cataracts, and while the operation was successful, the cure has been very slow. I hope very soon to be at Staten Island again, and you may rest assured you will be among the first upon whom I will inflict my society. I expect to join the club's social and hope you will permit me to be your escort to at least one or two of them, if not all of them. I have been asked to join the dancing class, but I am not sure whether I will do so. Still I am considering it. I am told that Jack and Marie's engagement is announced, and I wish them joy—they are such a jolly little pair.

Sincerely,
Will Batchelder

*   *   *   *

In spite of the fact that I had rejected numerous suitors and was an old maid of thirty-one, Trude always remained anxious for me to mix with the gentlemen, so that, like her, I could marry and start a family—in other words, become a conventional girl. Since my experience with gentlemen had been uniquely uninspired, I was not so anxious to look for a suitor, and therefore I had some trepidation about visiting the Eccleston family in the Catskills.

How foolish my fears were. The summer visit to Twilight Rest that year changed my life forever—and for the better. I did not meet a gentleman, but rather a lady: Miss Gertrude Amelia Tate of Brooklyn, New York. In the summer of 1897, I realized that although I would never marry, I would not be spending my life as a *lonely* spinster. I knew in my heart that Gertrude and I would be together for all of our lives. From the moment that I first saw Gertrude, I felt a warmth in my heart that was completely overwhelming. Other girls had described similar sensations when meeting young men, but until the day I first saw Gertrude, I believed that no one could stir such feelings in me. Certainly Mr. Carroll and Mr. Batchelder never had, despite their urgent efforts in that direction.

When I sat down with the other girls upon my arrival at Twilight Rest, Gertrude's lovely blue eyes locked firmly on mine, and the smile that lit up her face felt like the sunshine as it breaks through the clouds on a dark and dismal day. It is not too much to say that I was stunned. As I lie here over half a century later, I remember that moment as though it were yesterday, and the miracle of it is that I knew at the time that my first glimpse of Gertrude was the moment I fell in love.

So much of my life up to that moment seemed to fall into place and perspective. I had been looking (albeit halfheartedly) for a lifelong partner among the gentlemen and had found no one, but it was crystal clear to me by the end of that summer trip that Gertrude was the only person who I could ever love deeply enough to build a life with. It is true that I had loved other women—I know that I had been in love with Trude, for instance. In retrospect I know that the photograph I made of us in our slips and masks obviously had a special significance for me. When we took that photograph, I described my idea to Trude and said that it was just a lark—a humorous pose. The idea of tarting ourselves up like street girls was all mine, and Trude was rather reluctant to let herself go, even in such a private setting. But it was amusing to me and somewhat exciting, perhaps. I managed to persuade Trude to go along, and after all was said and done, she seemed to enjoy it as much as I.

I had been fascinated by the idea that by simply altering our manner of clothing, we could appear to be something that we were not and express feelings we were not accustomed to voicing. It was as if dressing like a woman of the lower classes could stimulate new sensations in me. At the moment we posed for that photograph, I remember feeling something for Trude that was more exciting than the love of friendship. It was a feeling I knew was best not to voice. Be that as it may, while Trude found the picture humorous, she seemed more embarrassed by it than anything else. She never took a print of the plate for herself and never wanted me to show the picture to even our closest friends. If I had to pinpoint my first feelings of love for another woman, the woman would be Trude. However, as I well know, Trude did not feel the same as I did. She recognized the depth of my feeling for her, and I think it frightened her. We never spoke of it. Over the years, we have drifted away from one another. She has never visited me here, although I believe she is still alive, hale and heartier than I. I can bear no grudges toward her—our lives simply took different paths.

*   *   *   *

So many friends have come and gone throughout the years. Some married, and others were more like me and did not. A few were like me and married anyway—Jessie MacNamee Simmons springs to mind. For many years, I had been a friend of Jessie's sister, Faith, and it was through Faith that I met Jessie. I was lukewarm about Faith—she was always so interested in the boys—but it was different with Jessie; we shared an interest in athletics and outings with the other girls (but not the boys), and over time we became very close. In later years, Gertrude and I often socialized with Jessie.

Jessie never professed much of an interest in the rituals of courtship, but I suppose Jessie fell victim to the social conventions, so she married and had one child. We had all learned as children that the ideal woman was one who devoted herself to the home, to her husband and her children—not all of us believed we were suited to that life, but we were not like those radical women who were popular in certain circles, Charlotte Perkins Gilman and Antoinette Blackwell. I had read in the newspaper about meetings where these women and others like them spoke out against common social wisdom, and none of my set approved of such vocal displays. Besides, if women did not take responsibility for creating a warm home atmosphere and for educating the children in proper behavior, society would suffer, and chaos would ensue. Some of us felt we were not suited to marriage, but we did not disagree that a woman's proper place was by the hearth. A woman's role has always been and still is today to raise children in a civilized and loving atmosphere, so the boys can become proper members of the business world and so that the girls can follow in their mothers' footsteps. The future of our race and of our great country depends on it. Civilization cannot continue to develop if women do not keep proper homes.

At any rate, Jessie married, and she had a miserable time of it. Her feelings for men as a species were not a secret; if anyone brought up the topic, she would rage. Once her little nephew brought up the subject of having a large family, and she told him flat out that the subject of having a brood of children and a husband by the hearth could not be discussed in her presence. I cannot say I felt differently from my friend about the male sex in general, given my experience with my ne'er-do-well and absent father, but my association with Uncle Pete, Uncle Oswald, and Papa tempered my reactions and, unlike Jessie, I was able to maintain cordial and warm relationships with certain gentlemen.

Eventually Jessie was widowed—which she considered a blessing, I think—and I do believe that no man ever entered her home again, except to do repairs. She had a lovely farm here on Staten Island that I often photographed. Jessie loved hostessing large gatherings, so we often had picnics and parties there, and the guests were always all women. I remember one party in particular; it was sometime after the turn of the century, but before the Great War. Only women were in attendance, and most of us dressed as men. Two of the girls were sailors; Jessie wore her jodhpurs and carried a riding crop, and I must say I looked rather spiffy in my mustache and knickers. I often wonder if I didn't look better as a man than as a woman. I certainly felt very comfortable dressed as one, but I do know I would never have wanted to be a man—the mere thought gives me goose bumps.

Over the years, Gertrude and I had many friendships with women who lived with other women and men who lived with other men—"homosexuals," the psychiatrists would call them these days. In my day, when we spoke of such things at all, we sometimes called them "bohemian" friends. We never thought about homosexuality; we just thought of ourselves as loving someone who happened to be of our same sex. Today the doctors make it sound like a disease, but we never even gave it a second thought—it was just how it was, something different and maybe a little exotic, but not a sickness.

Most of our bohemian friends lived in Greenwich Village, and we would go to their homes to socialize or out to dinner in the city. Gertrude and I never had them to our home; our Staten Island friends and neighbors would have been scandalized by some of their behavior—especially of the men, who often liked to dress in women's clothing and take the part of the lady with their friend. Somehow when we girls dressed up as men, it seemed amusing, but when the gentlemen dressed as ladies, it seemed scandalous.

Gertrude and I never pretended our relationship was anything other than it was. We traveled together and eventually we shared a home, but we were very quiet about our lives. We certainly didn't go around shouting our love and devotion from the treetops—our private life was strictly our private affair, and we did certain things to keep appearances. Although Gertrude and I usually shared the same bed, I always kept my separate bedroom downstairs. Gertrude took my grandparents' spacious room upstairs, with its big bed and fireplace, and when we first lived in the house together, we spent many joyful hours wrapped in each other's tender embrace. Gertrude's mother and her eldest sister, Carrie, recognized Gertrude's love for me and mine for her, and they did not approve. They were constantly telling Gertrude that she would never marry if she insisted on traveling about with "that old maid, Miss Austen." Gertrude and I used to laugh about that one. It would have been difficult for Gertrude to defy her mother and sister if she hadn't had the support of her other sister, Winifred, and Winifred's husband, who gave quiet acceptance of our relationship.

As for *my* family, well…they remained perfectly silent as they watched our relationship grow. They may not have approved—in fact they surely would have rather seen me married—but at least they made no comment to Gertrude or to me. There was gossip of course, but c'est la vie, and we chose not to dignify it by responding to it, either to confirm or deny.

We have loved each other for over fifty years, and we lived together for over thirty years. The only thing that truly matters is that our love for each other makes us content.

Dearest Julia,

The most remarkable thing has happened. I have a new crush, but it is oh-so-much more than a crush. I have met the most tender and loving and lovely creature in Miss Gertrude Amelia Tate. Oh, how shall I describe her? She is an angel, so delicate, so feminine, and so beautiful. Miss Tate teaches dance and deportment to help support her widowed mother, and she moves with the grace of an angel. Her eyes are the palest of blues, and through them I feel I can see the light of her perfect soul. When she smiles, she lights up the darkness. When she laughs, it makes the birds sing and the flowers bloom. Miss Tate is a perfect angel. She is the woman who was meant for me. And I believe she returns the feeling.

Each morning we walk on the trails for a short while; Miss Tate is recovering from a serious illness which nearly took her life (oh, G_d forbid!), so we take easy walks and then return to the piazza, where we sit in the rocking chairs and talk and laugh and silently gaze into one another's eyes while listening to the rustling trees and the rushing streams. You know how I am, dear Julia, rushing about from one activity to another. Not so this summer. I am perfectly contented sitting beside this dear lady. I feel that should I be so fortunate as to be able to sit beside Gertrude for my whole life, I should be the luckiest girl in the world. She is a wonder, and I cannot say enough. But you shall see for yourself if you visit the island ever again, because I know that my love—yes, my love—of this lady shall grow and continue for as long as I draw a breath. So should you return home fifty years hence, Gertrude and I shall still sit side by side in love and devotion.

I shall send you some photographs of this remarkable woman after I return home, so you will see for yourself her beauty. I only wish you could hear the beauty in her voice and feel the warmth in her eyes. My photographs cannot do this lady justice.

I feel that this letter says so little, because it is so brief, but I am so taken with my beautiful lady that I cannot sit idly alone for long. I promise I shall write you again soon. And how are things in Santa Barbara? Your boardinghouse sounds like a remarkable adventure. I do not like that we are so far away from one another, making exchange of confidences diffi-cult, but I am happy that you seem to be doing so well.

With love always,
Alice

*   *   *   *

My lovely Gertrude was on the verge of becoming engaged when we met. As the youngest of three sisters, Gertrude had put off setting a date for her marriage until her middle sister married, so as not to cause embarrassment for the elder sibling. At the least that was the excuse she had given her fiancé, Guy Loomis, for refusing to make a final commitment to him. When Gertrude and I met in 1897, she was twenty-six years old (five years younger than I) and living with her mother and middle sister, Winifred, in Brooklyn.

Her eldest sister, Carrie, was already married and living nearby. I would say "happily living nearby," but Carrie was always a great sourpuss—I don't think she was ever cheerful about anything, and I know that she disliked me because I stole Gertrude's heart. I have to laugh when I think of that old biddy with her pursed-up mouth puttering around while Gertrude and I visited in the family's Brooklyn apartment.

Most of the time, Gertrude would try to visit with me on the island, but this was not always convenient, because my Gertrude was a working girl. Gertrude's mother was a widow, and even though the old lady was as cheerful as oldest sister Carrie, Gertrude was devoted to her care. The family had absolutely no money and very little social standing, so both Gertrude and Winnie worked to put food on the table and to buy clothes. I can't recall what Winnie did before she married, but before Gertrude came to live on Staten Island with me in 1917, she was a teacher at the St. Bartholomew's Church Kindergarten on Madison Avenue at Forty-Fourth Street in New York City, and she made additional money by teaching deportment and ballroom dancing to youngsters. Gertrude was then (and still is) the picture of grace and good manners. She has a spirit that can only be described as light and beautiful. She is, in every sense of the word, a lady. Was it any wonder that a gentleman like Guy Loomis was enamored with her and yet was willing to wait for her to decide the proper time to officially announce their engagement?

In the summer of 1896, Gertrude was struck by a mysterious illness, which left her bedridden for months on end. After she recovered—almost as suddenly and mysteriously as she had become ill—she was severely weakened, and she had lost a great deal of weight and all of her hair. Gertrude's physician suggested a rest in the mountains to enhance her recuperation. That is how Gertrude came to spend the summer at Twilight Rest. Her bad luck in becoming seriously ill thus became our good fortune by giving us the opportunity to meet. The four weeks that we spent together in the Catskills flew by. We took walks in the woods, dreamily observing the beauties of nature, and I took countless photographs. Gertrude was unable to engage in physical activity due to her illness, so I refrained from my usual hectic pace that normally would have included long hikes on the forest trails, bathing, and sailing. Gertrude and I spent hours talking and rocking in the rocking chairs on the piazza, or resting on the nearby rocks by the waterfall, listening to the sounds of rushing water in the Catskill mountain streams. Normally sitting so still would have seemed stultifying, and I would have longed to rush headlong into physical activity and record each detail with my camera. But that summer, simply sitting beside Gertrude was enough to occupy my mind. When the day came for us to part, we promised to keep in touch, and Gertrude promised to visit me at my Staten Island home, which she did. When she could not visit me, I traveled to Brooklyn to see her at her mother's.

Gertrude Tate
Brooklyn, New York
10 October 1897

Dearest Alice,

We have been apart just twenty-four hours, and already my heart aches for your tender touch. I long for you with my whole being. The time that we share is precious and oh so short, but glorious.

I am so happy you were able to stay the weekend with us, but I must apologize for my mother, who makes no secret of her opinion that my time is better spent socializing with our little circle of girls and gentlemen, especially Mr. Loomis. She is anxious to see me marry well, and given our circumstances, I fully understand. However, I know now that I have met you, dear Alice, that the state of matrimony is not for me. You are the person I wish to spend my life with. Your touch and your embrace are all I need in life. As we curled around one another in my little girlhood bed, I felt safe and secure and warm. You are a gift, dear Alice, and I fear that words are inadequate to express the depth of my feelings.

I do hope we shall see each other soon. I am your devoted and loving friend always and forever.

Gertrude

---

12 October 1897
Alice Austen
Rosebank, Staten Island

My beloved Gertrude,

I had not yet had time to write my note of thanks to you and your mother when Mama handed me your note. I am so moved. I have felt the same about you as you feel about me, but I dared not express it in words for fear of overwhelming your sensibilities. As I lay beside you at night and held you tight in my arms I sensed there was nothing more in this world that I needed—you were everything and all things. During the daylight hours we had such a jolly time visiting with your friends, but the nights were pure bliss. I do not know how someone I have known for such a short time could become so important in my life, but I do know that you have. I fear that I cannot live another day without you.

Oh, how I wish we could be together always. But I know you have your responsibilities to your family, and now that must come first. I do hope those little children at the kindergarten appreciate their opportunity to spend so many waking hours in the presence of an angel such as you, dear Gertrude. They should feel themselves blessed.

When shall we be together again? I hope that someday soon you will be able to come visit me on the island. I so want you to meet my family and friends, and Trude longs to see you as well. Perhaps you will have some vacation in the near future that would permit an extended stay. I long to be with you, my angel.

Yours ever and always,
Alice

*   *   *   *

That was the beginning. Eventually Winnie was married, and Mr. Loomis asked my Gertrude to set a wedding date and officially announce their engagement. After some prodding on Mr. Loomis's part, Gertrude, with some exasperation, told her fiancé that she could no longer give him a commitment of any sort. She laughed when she told me later what she had said: "I cannot set a date; I am planning to go abroad with Alice." Mr. Loomis finally understood that a wedding was not in the cards for him and Miss Gertrude Tate. Once he recovered from the stunning news, he was definitely a gentleman about the rejection, and Gertrude and I were able to maintain a close friendship with him throughout our years together.

*   *   *   *

I had developed a habit over the years of preparing albums of photographs to give as gifts to people with whom I felt especially close. I have made books for Aunt Minn, Mama, my grandparents, and several close friends. I take care with these projects to ensure that each one is appropriate for the recipient. And I think of the gifts as a way to express my feelings and love for the person for whom I make them. Immediately after returning home from Twilight Rest that summer, I went to my closet darkroom on the second floor of our home and began the lengthy and tedious task of developing my glass plates and of making prints from specially selected negatives. Naturally Gertrude was a favored subject of my photographs as I sought to preserve the precious memories of that first summer together. At first Gertrude had been reluctant to pose due to her weakened physical state, but as the weeks progressed, she became more willing. She even posed for me without the wig she wore to cover her baldness. To me her willingness to expose this physical anomaly was a symbol of the intimacy that had developed between us in such a short time.

For days and nights after I returned home, I devoted my attention to selecting plates that would be appropriate to give Gertrude and that would convey the strength and depth of my feelings for her. Most of the pictures that I chose were of all the girls in various poses on the piazza and in the surrounding woods. I also included a portrait of Gertrude in her rocker with her wig on and one with her wig off. I felt these two images taken together made it clear how much we enjoyed ourselves that summer and how close we became. I mounted the prints in a leather-bound album and wrote an inscription in the front: "For GAT: There is nothing in this life that gives me more pleasure than the memory of our first summer together. Affectionately, EAA." I remember those words so clearly, because they were and still are the truth.

Chapter Four

Anna Forsyth
Secretary to H. Winthrop
1841 Broadway
New York, New York
February 5, 1950

Dear Mr. Winthrop,

As you requested before you left on your winter vacation, I arranged a visit to the Old Farm Colony on Staten Island, where I chatted with your cousin, Miss Austen. I like her very much, as you know, and I do believe she likes me. She has quite a sense of humor and is full of the devil in spite of her infirmities. She told me that when everyone is asleep, she gets out of bed with her cane and walks all over the first floor. She goes to the bathroom herself, which the nurses do not allow in the daytime, and then she goes back to bed, with no one the wiser.

In spite of the fact that the Farm Colony is so dreary, Miss Austen seems to be happier here than at the other two nursing homes she was at previously. She says the food is good, and while the routine is dreadful, she appreciates that, for the most part, the nurses and whatever doctors there are leave her alone.

I think your cousin is quite a tigress, and Miss Tate, who was also visiting the last time I was there, seems a little afraid of and in awe of Miss Austen. I do not know how they have maintained a friendship for so long. Miss Tate is such an angelic lady, and Miss Austen is so feisty. I do believe she could run a marathon with her canes and run races in her wheelchair. I suppose that since Miss Austen never married, Miss Tate provided the company and the sense of family that a lady who never married lacks. They do seem devoted to one another.

I do hope this letter finds you in improved health, Mr. Winthrop.

Your devoted secretary,
Anna Forsyth

*   *   *   *

I despise the days that that dreadful Miss Forsyth from Cousin Harry's office comes by to visit. As lonely as I feel sometimes, I would prefer no company to her sour face and high-pitched voice. And I know she rejoices at my misfortune, the old prude. Nothing gives a working girl a better laugh than seeing a once well-off lady in dire straits.

I think Miss Forsyth believes she is a good and devoted friend, but truth be told, I hardly know the woman, and therefore I see her as an acquaintance and as an employee of my cousin Harry. She asks thousands of questions regarding my health and conditions at the Farm Colony, and as a lady, I try to be polite, but if that woman thinks I would share a true thought or feeling with her, she is sadly mistaken. Some things should never be discussed, even obliquely, outside of one's immediate and closest society. And in my life now, my only family is my beloved Gertrude. Miss Forsyth is of class that neither understands the value of privacy nor appreciates that other people do value it. I should never engage in an open and frank discussion with a woman of Miss Forsyth's social standing, but I am too much of a lady to tell her that directly. So I tolerate her chatter and am civilly correct.

My relationship with Gertrude has been the solid rock foundation of my adult life. Without this beautiful lady, my life would have had its fulfillments, but I would not be completely fulfilled. It is certain that when my "courtship" of Gertrude began—and it began in earnest the moment I met her—no one in my family, nor anyone in her family, understood our feelings toward one another. Gertrude told me her sister and mother protested that if she continued to spend so much time with me, she would never find a husband. I think they thought me to be some mesmerizing serpent that was stealing the baby of the family and dragging her into a life of degradation that would eventually lead to ostracism from society.

In the era when Gertrude and I came of age, certain things were expected of a young lady if she were to be considered a true Lady, with a capital L. In school girls learned the social graces and domestic arts, and I was no exception here. My mother insisted that I attend the Miss Errington School for Young Ladies— where, in addition to reading and sums, I learned deportment, etiquette, and dancing, as well as several domestic arts: cooking, needlework, and miniature painting. A young lady's entire education was directed toward the single goal of preparing her for courtship and marriage. Girls in my set never considered the possibility that they would go out into the business world themselves. A proper young lady would meet a proper gentleman who would be capable of supporting his family without the assistance of his wife or children. This would not only allow a lady to create a proper home, but would also permit her to raise her children with the values of our society, so that they could be passed down from generation to generation. So I learned from Mama and Grandmother that a lady does not work. Rather, a lady should marry and have children.

It was also understood that there was a corollary to these social rules, and that while many people, including Mama and Aunt Minn, lived lives that to the public eye seemed above reproach and in line with convention, their public lives were not always a reflection of the truth of their situation. Of course Mama had been abandoned by my father, and that could have been quite a scandal, had the details of it been made public. However, when Mama was forced to answer about her husband's whereabouts, she said he had been lost at sea on his way to England. When Aunt Minn's first husband, Mr. Samuel Hicks, died, she quite quickly became involved in a courtship with Uncle Oswald, who had been the captain of the ship on which Aunt Minn and Mr. Hicks were sailing at the time of Mr. Hicks's demise. This clearly had an air of scandal about it, but it was kept quite quiet, and no one besides immediate family members and close friends was privy to the details. This is how I came to understand that a lady did not actually have to live according to the rules of society, but she had to give the appearance of doing so. In other words, a lady's private life must remain private.

I knew by the time I fell in love with Gertrude that if I did not marry a gentleman, Mama would see this as defiance of the normal ways of our society. But I also knew that I could maintain my reputation within my society if I were discreet about the nature of my relationship with Gertrude. And I certainly intended to be discreet, since I had been taught and firmly believed that whatever one does in the privacy of one's home should never be made public. No lady can afford a scandal. The maintenance of discretion in one's private life is what separates members of my set from members of the lower classes, who lived free and easy lives, which they conducted in the streets and the dives of their fetid neighborhoods. I wanted to do nothing in my life that would give the appearance of bringing me to that level. My entire life has been guided by the idea that a lady behaves in certain ways, and I will not give up my principles simply because I have taken an oath of poverty.

No one besides Gertrude and myself was ever privy to the intimate nature of our relationship. I am sure that no one, not even our closest friends, knew how Gertrude and I kissed each other on the lips and held each other on dark nights before going to sleep. It makes me laugh when I think of that prude Miss Forsyth saying to my beautiful Gertrude, "Oh, what a devoted friend you are; you are more devoted than a wife would be to a husband or a husband to a wife." She truly believes that Gertrude and I were two old spinster ladies who lived together for thirty years to share expenses, and that our devotion to one another was purely sisterly.

My relationship with Gertrude aside, my life for the most part followed the traditional path of young girls of my generation and class. As a young girl, I developed many interests. I was always extremely athletic, so I participated in all kinds of activities. I loved bathing in the bay in front of our home, and when tennis became popular, I became an avid and accomplished player. When I was quite young, Uncle Oswald and Uncle Pete taught me how to sail, and Papa even bought me my own small sailing boat. I was one of the first young women to take up bicycling and was a member of the Staten Island bicycling club. Daisy Elliott and the Ward sisters, Carrie and Vi, and I would ride for hours on end all over the island.

Like Papa, I loved gardening. I think that gardening was one thing that saw me through the hard years. Even when I could barely walk because of arthritic stiffness, I tended to the garden myself. When the house fell into disrepair, I always managed to keep up our lovely flowers. My garden was like a pleasing dream. As I bent over the flowers and took in their beauty and fragrance, in my mind I would be transported to lovelier times—times when the pressures of money, unpaid bills, and undone repairs were not a concern.

In the colder months, when gardening and traveling about outside were impossible or impractical, I turned my attention to reading. I read periodicals having to do with photography and mechanical things, as well as women's books such as the *Ladies' Home Journal*, which often had articles on photography and album making. And I loved books about travel. Samuel Pepys's diaries were a favorite of mine. They reminded me of my tours of Europe with Gertrude. We traveled to France, where we had dresses and gloves and hats made for the fall opera season in New York. We traveled to the Netherlands, Switzerland, Germany, and England, visiting museums and traveling in the countryside by car and even by donkey. I loved to photograph the sights that we visited, and I loved to photograph Gertrude, and sometimes the two of us together. I miss those excursions away from home. As much as I love my home, traveling about with Gertrude always seemed to sharpen our love for one another. Perhaps it was that we were away from the distractions of our families and our usual friends. And of course it was our mutual enjoyment of the sights and sounds of foreign ports of call. Our trips were not as adventurous as Daisy Elliott and Carrie Ward's, but they were magical times.

Daisy and Carrie, daring souls that they were, once took a bicycling trip through-out Switzerland, Germany, and France, before I met Gertrude, and the letters they sent me made me wish I had the chance to take such a journey. They had asked me to travel with them, and I considered it, but declined to go in the end, because I had already committed myself to spending the month of August at Twilight Rest, and because I had also promised to participate in the tennis tour-naments here on Staten Island. I felt I could not justify backing out of my prior commitments, even for a tempting travel offer such as that one. It was a trip I wish I had shared—not just for the adventure, but for other reasons as well. It was the summer of 1897, and I had had a heartbreaking time over Carrie's sister, Violet. I had a tremendous crush on that girl, but my feelings were unrequited. At first it seemed as though Violet's feelings for me were similar to mine for her, but suddenly, without warning or explanation, she rejected me in the harshest and most public way by spurning my every invitation and snubbing me at other events. I was perplexed by her behavior and to this day have no explanation for it. Needless to say, I was more than a little bit jealous of my friends across the ocean. Of course, in retrospect, I am relieved that things did not go well between Violet and me, because 1897 was the summer that I met Gertrude at Twilight Rest. However, at the time, I was deeply hurt and thought that nothing could compen-sate for the terrible pain that Vi's rejection caused me.

18 July 1897
Daisy Elliott
Austria

Alice, dear one,

I found your letter on my arrival this afternoon, and though I am short of time, I felt the need to respond immediately to your distress. I have, as you requested, read over your letter twice and destroyed it, so rest assured on that account. I am sorry that things with said young woman are no better for you—it is entirely incomprehensible and outside the borders of rea-son. The more I think of it, the worse it seems—I cannot reconcile myself to her way of doing or understand it. It is unheard of and seems unneces-sary. If her feelings have changed, she owes you an explanation. Her com-plete silence on the matter is not only hurtful, but beyond the bounds of respectability. Of course, as you asked, I have said nothing here or asked any questions, although I do think Carrie may have insight into her sister's outrageous behavior toward you. I have not, however, heard a single word and have not written to Vi myself. I feel so helpless that there is nothing that I can do for you, dear one, as you have so often comforted and aided me in similar trials. It is the cruelest experience I have heard of in my life, and I wish I could ease it for you.

I shall close now, as I am anxious to make today's post, but shall write again when time permits. Carrie and I have had so many wondrous experiences, and I wish you were here to share them with us. Please write me also.

All my love and affection,
Daisy

*   *   *   *

Youth is often filled with pain, I suppose, but what I wouldn't give to be transported back to my youth, to its sorrows and its triumphs. I long to feel the joys—
and yes, even the heartaches—of youth: to travel and to play tennis and bathe in
the bay and sail my little ship. This poor farm is not so bad, but I do miss my privacy, my possessions, and even my crowded bedroom, where I kept so many
things that were dear to me. The shelves in my room contained a variety of trea-
sured travel guides. And of course, I read the newspapers daily; Gertrude used to
tease me, because I refused to throw them out. In the end, my room was so
stacked with old newspapers that one had to blaze a trail to find one's way
around. Gertrude said she was afraid she would lose me forever in that room.

Thoughts of Gertrude always bring me joy. Before I met her my life was a
confusion of feelings. My growing up was so difficult in so many ways. I was just
so different from the other girls. Although I loved to read, I was not enamored of
school, but when Mama insisted that I attend the Miss Errington School for
Young Ladies, I had no choice but to comply. I was not a willing student especially when it came to drills and following prescribed lessons. Sums eluded me,
and I was not terribly interested in learning the details of domestic life, such as
needlework and china painting. Dancing lessons were enjoyable, but deportment
classes were boring. I did like cooking, surprisingly; perhaps because I love a good
meal, as my constant battle with my weight makes clear. I had sometimes
dreamed of being wraithlike, but my appetite for good food always defeated me.

15 August 1888
Mrs. Austen
2 Pennsylvania Avenue
Rosebank

My dearest Lollie,

It was such a pleasant surprise to receive still another letter from you. It
was in the front hall when I returned from shopping in the city today. I was
perfectly exhausted from my trip to the dressmaker and from having luncheon with that perverse Mr. Gilman, who tries to win your heart with
invitations to your mother. Perhaps I should have declined, knowing how
you feel about his attentions, but as I was scheduled for a fitting this afternoon, I gave in to his pleadings. The meal was refreshing, but my companion was positively stifling.

I was most distressed by the tone of your letter, which seemed tinged with anger at yourself. I know you fancy that a wraithlike figure would become you, but in truth, I believe that your figure is quite satisfactory. You may say I tell you this because I am your mother and therefore am not an impartial judge, but I say this because it is true. It is clear that many of the gentlemen find your figure pleasing—witness the unrelenting Mr. Gilman. And I know you are the envy of many of the other young ladies. So do not despair, dear Loll, for in all ways, you are truly beautiful.

I hope this letter finds you in good spirits. All is fine with me.

Yours affectionately,
Mama

*   *   *   *

When I was seventeen, Miss Errington decided she was too old to teach young and spirited ladies (we could be a handful), so she closed the doors to her school. It was none too soon for me—learning to be a proper young lady was hardly my idea of an interesting way to pass the day. Free from the strictures of school, I was able to engage in athletics as I wished, and I was able to travel. At first I traveled to visit friends and family for the most part, but as I grew older, I traveled further afield—into Canada, as far west as Ohio, and south to the nation's capital.

21 August 1896
Alice Austen
Lake Mohonk, New York

Dearest Mama,

The whole month of August has virtually flown by, and I have neglected to write you. Can you ever forgive me? I have been so busy here at Lake Mohonk that I have had no time to sit and write, but today it is raining, so I can catch my breath. The Mountain House is a beautiful spot and well situated on Lake Mohonk. There is in fact a large piazza that actually overhangs the water, so one feels as though one is sitting on the lake. There is so much to do here, but mostly I have been playing tennis, cycling, and hiking on the many trails. The other day, we took an excursion to Lake Minnewaska, which is even more beautiful than Lake Mohonk. It is a glacial lake, so the water is perfectly clear. There are no fish, but unfortunately it is too cold for bathing.

I have had such a jolly time here with Trude, Trude's sister, Edith, and Edith's husband and three boys. Mr. Barton is here as well, and oh, how he dotes on Trude. My friends have been very patient with me as I stop to take pictures of all the beautiful scenes—and of course, you know me, I take more than one picture of each scene to make sure that I have a good exposure. Papa loved Lake Mohonk so, and I think of him as I wander through the woods and hills.

Next week, as you know, we have planned an excursion to Canada—Kingston, Ontario, to be exact—and I am looking forward to that event, as I have never traveled to Canada before. As you know, dear Mama, whenever I travel to new places, I feel compelled to take photographs of every sight and all the people that I see, so I must be sure to take enough glass plates with me on the journey.

I shall write you from Canada, Mama.

Your loving daughter,
Loll

---

8 September 1896
Alice Austen
Kingston, Ontario, Canada

Dearest Mama,

Just a quick note to say that all is fine with me. Kingston has been marvelous, and I am taking pictures of everything—the scenery, the fortifications at Advance Battery, and the people (the recruits, our friends, and even local people whom I do not know, but who pose for my camera happily).

I shall be home soon, and then to work in my darkroom. I have enjoyed myself so much on this trip that there are no words.

Yours lovingly,
Loll

*   *   *   *

My social life was very active; I was often invited to participate in tennis championships, picnics, dances, luncheons...and weddings, of course. One by one, almost all of my childhood friends married. I felt the pressure to marry as well, but none of the gentlemen ever interested me. And no man ever matched up to Gertrude. I am quite pleased that I never tied myself to a man in marriage. As much as I like children, marriage to any man would be simply too confining.

Not that it was a simple decision to not marry. I had a great deal of inner turmoil concerning my relationships with the many gentlemen I knew. As my friends married, there was a part of my heart that longed to follow in their footsteps, to be like them, to be like all the girls.

The single person I have loved in my life is my beautiful Gertrude, but at the same time I loved Gertrude, I was afraid of her—well, not of her precisely, but of my love for her. I was raised with the idea that someday I would marry and raise a family of my own, so in the back of my mind, my failure to follow the prescribed course always nagged. I felt, among other concerns, that I was cheating society of another generation of Austens and that I was somehow déclassé. I believed I was inadequate, because I could not do what all the other girls did. And I knew in my heart that while loving another woman was truly not a crime, society still *considered* it a crime against nature and against civilized life. Sometimes I saw myself as involved in the worst kind of debauchery. Sometimes I thought that perhaps my brain was defective. In my eyes, Trude and her sister, Edith Eccleston Blunt, were exemplars of true womanhood. And I was the opposite. But I did try to be a true woman, and Edith Blunt pushed me along. Edith was the elder of the two girls, and as such, she married first—and, having done so herself, she tried to assist Trude (successfully) and me (unsuccessfully) in securing proper husbands.

November 6, 1889
Edith Blunt
Fort Wadsworth
Staten Island, New York

My dear Alice,

I believe Trude spoke to you some time ago about an excursion that my husband, Colonel Blunt, has asked me to arrange to West Point for the Cadet's Thanksgiving Hop on Wednesday, November 27. Miss Raoul and Miss Alexander have agreed to join us, and we plan to travel up on Tuesday afternoon and return by dinnertime on Thanksgiving Day. Trude suggested that you may wish to join us as well. The cost of transportation and so on will be $7, and the commandant at West Point has promised me partners for all the girls whom I escort.

I do hope you will be able to join us; as you know, the gentlemen at West Point are very interesting and excellent dancers as well.

Yours affectionately,
Edith Eccleston Blunt

May 12, 1890
Trude Eccleston
Fort Douglas
Salt Lake City, Utah

Dear Alice,

Mama and I arrived here last week to visit Edith and the colonel. You have no idea what a long trip it is to this distant outpost, but in truth, it was exciting. The post is beautifully situated right at the foot of the snow-covered mountains. We have an exquisite view of the valley and the city below and also the lake, which is like an ocean and as blue as a sapphire. The girls who are visiting here now I do not like very much. They are too free and easy for my style and decidedly fast—but I await some of the girls from the island who are more to my liking.

That's enough about the girls; now for the men. I like all the officers so far. I could not help it, as they have all been so polite to me. If I have any preference, it is for the older bachelors, with one exception, perhaps: Mr. Grey, who is the adjutant and reminds Edith and me so much of the fine gentlemen that I have met back East. No one here matches the fine qualities of Mr. Barton, whom I look forward to seeing upon my return to the island. I am suspicious that the gentlemen on the base may be attracted to the Mormon religion, which permits more than one wife. That would definitely not be to my liking.

Do write and tell me about yourself during my long absence. I fear I am missing something when I am away from home for more than one week. Have you been introduced to anyone of particular interest during your round of spring socials?

With piles of love for your own dear self, I am your loving friend,
Trude Eccleston

*   *   *   *

Over the years, I did meet several gentlemen who would have made suitable marriage partners and who were interested in me. I do admit that unlike my friend Trude, I did not pursue the gentlemen with vigor. Trude went to visit her sister at the posts where the colonel was stationed: first Utah and then the Presidio in California. She was forever writing me about this "dear officer" and "that handsome officer." And of course she asked me to go with her. But I had no desire to travel vast distances in search of a husband. Seeking a suitable marriage partner was not my idea of an exciting adventure.

One summer when I was with Trude in the Catskills, at the age of twenty-six and well on my way to being a spinster, I was introduced to a gentleman by the name of Mr. Willie Hopper, and we did have quite a wonderful time together. Mr. Hopper, Trude, and I staged a series of photographs that summer. Mr. Hopper urged me to submit them to *Life*, a humor magazine at the time (not a picture magazine, as it is now). The pictures were quite a good joke. We posed on a grave marker that had the family name "Noyes," exposing either the "no" or the "yes." And we acted out a courtship and marriage proposal, the results of which were reflected in the word that was shown. We did have a wonderful time. Mr. Hopper and I also posed together for several humorous photographs depicting a courting couple on a picnic. I always wanted the final photograph to show the lady turning away the prospective suitor. Both Mr. Hopper and Trude, who posed for some of the photographs, wanted to have love triumph in the end. I suppose this was a matter of our different perspectives on the joys of love and marriage. Mr. Hopper said that he wanted no part of a "tragic finale."

What I did not realize at the time, or perhaps what I chose to ignore at the time, was that Mr. Hopper was falling for me. When I returned home, he besieged me with letters, none of which I answered.

August 31, 1892
Willie Hopper
Twilight Rest

Dearest Alice,

I hope you sent a set of the photographs from the cemetery to *Life*. I think they were quite funny—and as you said, an interesting observation of the way men and women perceive courtship and marriage. Of course, don't count me in on the proceeds from any sale—Trude and I were mere actors in a piece designed and staged by you. My reward would be in knowing you were published.

This place has been horribly slow without you, and I did wish you could have gotten back, but do not come now, for I leave, as previously remarked, on Saturday…

These diagonal blotches in the ink are tear points—fast colors my eyes are not, for they ran when the tears ran over them. This is awfully mixed, but you know what it is to write when one is struck in the heart. Now please do not write me any more messages through Miss Eccleston's letters, but write me directly. I assure you that I love you more than ever, believe me.

Very affectionately,
Your own Willie

*   *   *   *

As smitten as Mr. Hopper was with me, I do believe that Mr. Henry Gilman, a business acquaintance of Uncle Pete's, was even more so. Mr. Hopper realized quite swiftly that I did not return his feelings and gave up the chase. But Mr. Gilman pursued me relentlessly—and I might add, pathetically—for years. He constantly sought invitations to my home and repeatedly invited me to this or that social function in New York. At first I accepted, because he seemed like a suitable marriage prospect (he was very attentive to Mama and Grandmother), but after a time, for my own sanity, I put him off.

*   *   *   *

24 September 1889
Henry Gilman
The Players Club
16 Grammercy Park
New York, New York

Dear Miss Austen,

I am sorry to have missed the note you sent me this past August inviting me to the club dance, but I had not checked my box here at the club, as mail is usually sent to me at my father's home in Flushing or at my place of employ, 10 Wall Street. I do hope you have not given up on me, as I do wish to see you again. I was thinking perhaps that you and your dear mother would enjoy some kind of mild spree, which would include a trip to the theatre and some kind of celebratory dinner at the Lawyer's Club. Please let me know if that is agreeable to you so that we can set a date. I will be going to Chicago next week for a divorce case, so I would like to make arrangements before then.

With kindest regards to your family,
Henry K. Gilman

November 2, 1891
Henry Gilman
103 Montague Street
Brooklyn, New York

My dear Miss Austen,

Oh, how I long to see you again on these dreary autumn days, for you are a spot of glorious sunshine. I think a sight of you would help me shake off a desperate attack of the blues, which seems to have fastened its demoralizing clutches upon me, and I wish you would drop me a line to say which evening this week I shall find you disengaged. I am living at 103 Montague Street now, and my evenings are free to the pitch of absolute loneliness, so do take pity on a poor, grubbing, desolate soul, and lay up for yourself treasures in heaven by a charitable action, and experience the highest pleasure in life by making another's lot in life less dreary.

With sincerest affection,
Henry K. Gilman

November 23, 1891
Henry Gilman
103 Montague Street
Brooklyn, New York

Dear Miss Austen,

I was heartbroken that you were forced to cancel our appointment, but I do understand that the stresses of life can cause a delicate soul such as yourself to experience an ache in the head. But please be aware that not seeing you causes an ache in my heart. Perhaps you will be so kind as to choose another evening at your convenience for me to visit with you.

With a longing heart and sincerest affection,
Henry Gilman

July 18, 1892
Henry Gilman
1441 Broadway
New York, New York

My dear Miss Austen,

How fortunate you are! Imagine a trip all the way to Chicago to see the Columbian Exposition. I hear it is one of the great fairs of all time, and I was delighted to hear that you are embarking on yet another adventure. But I am saddened that once again this means I shall not have an opportunity to have my eyes light on your luminous visage. Although it would be a small consolation, perhaps you would be so kind as to send me a portrait of yourself and your address this summer in the event that I might have the opportunity to write—or better still, visit you. The mere thought of this possibility brightens my day.

It might interest you to know that I am making quite a success of myself as the receiver of rent profits and issues. I do hope this pleases you, for it is for you that I make every effort to be a successful gentleman. As this is the case, I must keep my nose to the grindstone. And I am hoping my reward will be an evening with you upon your return.

I apologize if this letter is choppy, but I am constantly interrupted and am always somehow in a rush.

Hastily yours my dear lady,
Henry Gilman

July 3, 1893
Henry Gilman
The Players Club
16 Grammercy Park
New York, New York

Dear Miss Austen,

I meant to send you a line but found that I had no letter paper at the office—forgot to get some Friday and so postponed writing until today, hoping I should hear from you as to whether we could visit sometime soon. In your last letter to me, you sought to aggravate me, I think, by prattling on about your lovely moonlit nights with the ladies on your piazza. I am just dying for one myself, but fear I shall not get it unless I find a boarding place near your home in Rosebank on your lovely Staten Island for a few weeks. I suppose you will be enjoying yourself at the fair as I write this, and if I had passes for myself, I would rush out to be at your side, if only for a day. I have a good mind to do it as it is, but as you have neglected, once again, to let me know your address, I fear that I shall spend my short visit racing all over Chicago in hopes of catching a glimpse of you. I am enclosing a photograph of myself for you, but I am disappointed you have not sent me one of yourself as I requested. Please do not deny me any longer.

As always,
Henry Gilman

*   *   *   *

It was not that Mr. Gilman was an unsuitable gentleman—he came from a good family, he had a profession—and in fact was quite well-off for a young man. There was just something about him that troubled me, and I could never summon up strong feelings for the gentleman. After an ardent courtship of three years, he simply gave up (much to my relief). At the time, I felt that neither Mr. Gilman nor Mr. Hopper had the energy and the drive I had, and I did not believe I would be happy with either of them. But it took me some time to understand that it was not that these two gentlemen were sad examples of American manhood—which, in some respects, both of them were—that caused me to reject them. It was rather that I was the sort of woman who would never be fulfilled with a man. When I look back at the "no-yes" photographs that I made with Mr. Hopper and Trude, I see now that without being conscious of it, I was reflecting on and making a judgment regarding the relationship between men and women. All that I had learned in school and at home led me to believe that a happy marriage and family was a lady's ultimate goal. Many of my friends married and began families and seemed so happy, but while I appreciated their sense of fulfillment, and while I could see their joy, I thought this was not what I wanted in my own life. However, as a young woman, I knew that I wanted something, but I did not know what that was. It was through my friendships with other women like myself (Daisy, Jessie, Carrie, Vi, and, of course, Gertrude) that I realized what I was searching for.

Chapter Five

Mr. Oglesby's recent visit spurred me to think of all that I have had in my life and all that I have lost. My family was descended from a long line of distinguished Americans. Grandmother came from a family of Revolutionary War patriots, and so did Papa. Grandmother's ancestors were responsible for building the huge chain that General George Washington ordered placed across the Hudson River at West Point to prevent the English from sailing north. A link from that chain hung over the mantel in the parlor for many years. It went to that horrid Mr. Jaffee, despite my efforts to keep it from him by hiding it under my apron. It was simply too heavy for me, and although I had once been an athletic girl, at that time I was bent, and my hands had already become gnarled with arthritis.

Papa was able to make a very comfortable home for all of us. He and his younger brother, Uncle David Austen, were in business together, having taken over and expanded their father's business when they were young men. They were involved in the importing and selling of dry goods from a warehouse in Manhattan. The income that Papa acquired from his business and from his inheritance enabled our entire family to live a life of relative ease for all the years of my childhood. I regret having had to give that up. I miss my home terribly, and I wish that Gertrude and I were still sharing a life under the same roof. For so many years, Gertrude and my home were at the center of life.

---

14 February 1918
Alice Austen

Dearest Angel Gertrude,

I leave this Valentine upon your pillow as a symbol of my everlasting devotion to you. The sun rises and sets on you, my darling, and there is no greater joy than the joy I have found in you.

Do you realize we have known each other over twenty-one years...and still each morning, when I see your sleeping face, I feel the same thrill that I felt the first time I saw it at your home in Brooklyn so many mornings ago? We have lost so many people dear to us in our lives, and yet I feel as though with you I have everything. I know we are blessed to be together under one roof. At long last, I can wake each morning and find you beside me, and I can close my eyes at night, safe in your warm and tender embrace. I can kiss your pale blue eyes and your beautiful mouth at any moment during the day. I love to gaze on your beautiful face over the breakfast table. I love to comb out your soft and sensuous white hair each night. Please, my dear, do not ever think of cutting it—it is a reminder each night that you are truly an angel and that I am truly blessed.

On this our first Valentine's Day together in *our* home, I thank whatever fate has brought us together. It is you, dearest Gertrude, whom I love and whom I cherish. And I need nothing but you to make my life complete.

With everlasting love,
Alice

2 January 1950
Gertrude Tate
Jackson Heights, Queens, New York

Dearest Alice,

I do hope you will be able to read my handwriting. It is difficult to write now, as my vision is clouded by glaucoma. But I did so want to wish you a happy New Year and a happy new decade. I cannot believe we have entered the second half of the twentieth century, although it does seem eons since we left the nineteenth century behind. I do miss you, dear Alice, and long for the days when we were together. You know that my love for you never fades and will surely never die. I do hope to visit you soon.

Things here at Winnie's are fine, and my nephew Tate has been by to visit. He did ask after you; he still calls you his "Aunt Al." How that amuses me, and I think that you know why.

I hope this letter finds you in good spirits.

Yours lovingly and devotedly,
Gertrude

*   *   *   *

I had so many good friends over the years that have slowly drifted away—friends who were there to support me as I was coming to terms with the fact that my crushes on girls lingered long after the age when it was considered appropriate, and long after my crushes should have turned to the gentlemen. If I had to identify one woman who showed me through her example that a lady can find ways to be a lady without marriage, it would be Julia Martin. Julia left Staten Island when we were both in our early twenties under rather dark circumstances. Although we saw each other infrequently after she left home, Julia and I corresponded by letter weekly for a decade until she moved to California. There was so much about our lives that was different, yet we were so close in so many ways, in spite of the fact that Mama did not exactly approve of our association. I do not truly understand the source of Mama's disaffection for Julia—whether it was due to her father's treachery or Julia's way of life.

When Julia and I became acquainted, Julia's family was well respected, and Julia's father was considered a man of some substance. But although Mr. Martin was well-off, Papa was suspicious of his method of acquisition. Papa and his brother Uncle David worked daily in the city at their dry goods and importing business, and therefore their income—and, of course, their inherited wealth—was come by honestly. But Mr. Martin was something of a speculator, investing heavily in the stock market and in ventures that, while seemingly successful, were suspect in nature. People often said that his wealth came from "robbing Peter to pay Paul" schemes.

Julia and her family lived in a very comfortable and lovely home in a fashionable Staten Island neighborhood. In fact I was so taken with the Martin home that it was one of the first subjects outside my own home that I photographed extensively. The Martins, like Trude's family, had a summer cottage at Twilight Rest, and that is where Julia and I became close friends. We took long walks on the trails together, exchanging our ideas on so many topics, but especially gentlemen and marriage. Neither one of us was interested in the domestic side of life. We both agreed that while all the other girls became engaged, we were happy at the prospects of becoming old maids. The word "spinster" held no terror for us, but the word "wife" certainly did.

Twilight Rest was a lovely resort in a beautiful setting, but Mr. Martin thought that something more elegant would be popular with our set, so he set about acquiring property of his own in the mountains near Bennington, Vermont. He drew up detailed plans for an elegant hotel perched on a mountaintop that would be reached by an incline railroad. Mr. Martin called his resort Camp Comfort. That name irked Papa, because he felt that Mr. Martin had stolen his idea from our family, since Grandmother had called our home Clear Comfort.

Mr. Martin did not have the financial wherewithal to finance Camp Comfort on his own, so he set about asking friends and acquaintances on Staten Island and in Vermont to invest in this scheme. Papa was asked but refused, much to Mr. Martin's anger and dismay. Papa told us that Mr. Martin's plan was "risky at best." How prescient those words proved to be, for soon after the project got under way, it went bankrupt. Mr. Martin came under investigation by the authorities, who determined that there had been financial irregularities and called on Mr. Martin to return whatever monies he could to investors. Of course, there was no money with which to reimburse anyone, so the Martins lost everything, including their beautiful home on Staten Island.

To add insult to injury, Mr. Martin ran out on his family, leaving them to whatever the fates had in store. Our entire family felt badly for Julia and Mrs. Martin, who were truly victims of Mr. Martin's perfidy and who were left virtually homeless. Julia and her mother leased a small house but were unable to meet the payments. Meanwhile Mr. Martin disappeared from view for several years. With no home of her own after eviction from the leased house, Mrs. Martin put many of her possessions in storage in friends' homes, including ours, and went to live with a series of old friends of the family. Julia, who was grown, but of course not married, traveled about with her mother, but as funds became short, Julia went out in the world to seek employment. In later years, Mama often saw Mr. Martin on Staten Island; he had managed to recover some of his wealth and made an attempt to reenter society. His attempts were futile. No one could ever forget that he was a schemer, and so he never was a true gentleman. Perhaps if he had done something to help Julia's mother or Julia herself, he might have been reconsidered. But his return to financial wealth could not undo the damage he had done to the entire family's respectability.

Perhaps Mama never really approved of Julia because her father's treachery cast a pall over the entire family, but more likely, Mama did not approve of Julia because of the life she led. After losing her home, Julia became something of a vagabond—first visiting with friends in Baltimore and then moving to Albany, then to Vermont, then back to Albany again, and ultimately, Santa Barbara, California.

Julia Martin
c/o M. Barnett
1220 N. Calvert Street
Baltimore
6 May 1890

My dear Alice,

Though I have not much time, I am going to write to you, because I know you will be glad to hear from me, and I hope to hear from you soon. Please do not get lonesome. I am truly sorry to have gone off now and left you—that isn't said for effect at all, but is pure truth.

I went up to the city on Tuesday in all that rain to say farewell to some dear friends. I left for here early yesterday morning. Mrs. Barnett and Ruth met me at the station, and I had a very warm reception from all, which was quite a pleasant change from the coldness I felt on the island. I am to stay here ten days, which hardly seems enough, but then I will travel with my mother to see Mrs. Snively in Vermont, and then to see the McHargs in Albany for the coldest winter months. So things seem to be going well enough for now. I do not know what we will do after our visit with the McHargs. It seems as though we cannot live off the kindness of our friends forever.

I must close now so with love, believe me, ever,
Lovingly,
Julia T. Martin

∗   ∗   ∗   ∗

I know that Mama did not approve of how outspoken Julia was in her views on marriage. Mama made it quite clear to me that after Julia moved away, she hoped I would not see her anymore. Sometime after Julia moved to the McHargs' in Albany, she returned to the city to tidy up some business of her mother's. She wrote and asked to visit our home. As I was away at Uncle Pete's in New Jersey at the time her letter arrived, Mama forwarded Julia's note to me, along with a note of her own urging me not to cut my visit with Uncle Pete short in order to see Julia.

20 September 1891
Mrs. Austen
2 Pennsylvania Avenue
Rosebank

My dearest Lollie,

I was very glad to get your card so soon. I was anxious to know that you were settled at Uncle Pete's and that your trunk had arrived with you.

I have enclosed a card from Julia Martin that arrived at about six o'clock on Saturday. You see, she wants to come on Thursday next. This you must not let her do, for it would quite break up your outing, which is short enough as it is. Besides I had hoped that you would have an opportunity to visit with your cousin, Emmie Van Rensselaer, in Fishkill if possible, directly after your visit with your uncle. Julia has kept you in uncertainty all summer until she was prepared to fix a date herself. She should not encourage you to change your vacation plans in order to accommodate her. Do stay in Bay Head as you had planned. I know that Julia seeks your comfort with her troubles, but one cannot live one's life for someone else. Julia should honor your feelings and desires, and not put her own above yours.

I have seen Mr. Martin on the ferry, and he shows a total disregard for manners, acting as though nothing has happened to alter his standing in society. Julia is behaving similarly.

I hope you are well, dear Lollie. Rest assured that all is fine with me.

Yours affectionately,
Mama

*   *   *   *

Much to Mama's dismay, I did cut my visit short with Uncle Pete in order to return home to visit with Julia, who stayed several days with us. Mama was not pleased, but as always she tried to maintain a polite attitude toward my guest. At times Julia did not make it easy for Mama. I recall that Julia, Mama, and I were discussing Faith MacNamee's engagement—that is, Jessie's sister—when Julia declared that she would never marry herself and that she preferred the company of women to the company of men. Julia made no secret of her crushes on other girls. She in fact said on several occasions that she would have made a fine man, because she was "better at making love" than any of the gentlemen with whom we had been acquainted. When we were young, all the girls had crushes on other girls, but when we reached marriageable age, it seemed inappropriate somehow. At least it did in Mama's eyes. But I understood and agreed with Julia completely. Like my friend, I could never understand why any girl would want to tie herself up with a gentleman. (How Mama didn't see this, I shall never know.) We were certainly as good as the men, if not better.

As if to draw a portrait of our opinion on the subject, one day Julia, Julie Bredt (who ardently agreed with our position against marriage), and I dressed ourselves up as men and posed for photographs. We wore pants, waistcoats, jackets, and hats, carried cigarettes, and struck a variety of jaunty and serious male poses. In one photograph, Julia, who was the most brazen and outspoken among us, was seated in the middle, between Julie and I, who stood on either side. Julia had her ankle resting on the opposite knee in a typical jaunty gentleman's pose. At the last moment, Julia took an umbrella and placed the handle in a sensitive area such that it resembled a male organ in a state of excitement. As Uncle Oswald pressed the shutter for us, we all could barely contain ourselves. Perhaps Mama noticed this when she saw the picture, and this is what set her off against Julia. My mother was not one who appreciated ribaldry. And in the main, I would agree with her. A lady does not discuss matters relating to sexual relations. I know that in some respects, it is different today—with young people freely talking about these things. But when I was young, it just was not done.

Julia Martin
c/o Mr. McHarg
23 Elk Street
Albany, New York
31 December 1891

My dear Alice,

I am sure you wonder if I have received the pictures. Thank you so much for them. They are perfectly splendid. What do you think? They came this morning while I was out at church. When I came in with Mrs. Snively and her mother, Mrs. Cooper, I found that Mrs. Snively's sons had opened them, and they were in full view of one and all. Of course everyone caught on. I was *wild*. Everyone asked who the good-looking gentlemen were, and of course everyone knew that it was you and I and Julie Bredt. Mrs. Snively and Mrs. Cooper thought you were the best. Have you sent a copy to Julie? She is such a brick. It was delightful to visit with all of you, although I wish I could have extended my stay at your home.

Alice, I hope that you will be able to visit me here, or perhaps in Bennington, should I be there, in the coming year, as I am quite lonely for your friendship. Our visit in Bennington last August was so enjoyable, and so was my visit to the island this past October. Do not get me wrong; there is plenty to interest me here, and I am happy to be far away from the stares and pointed fingers on Staten Island. Mama is physically much better than when we left, but mentally she is a wreck. I fear the treachery of my father will cause her mind to go completely. She does not sleep, but wanders about the house all night long, wringing her hands with worry and speaking unintelligible words. I have made up my mind that if Papa does not extend himself to help in another week, I shall take Mama to a hospital here in Albany.

All is not dismal here, and so I would be willing to stay on if the McHargs, who have taken us in once again for the winter months, will keep me while Mama recovers. Did I tell you that I have a new crush? She is Hattie Pruyn, and I have seen a good deal of her. She was in church this morning and had a rose in her hat, but she was more beautiful than the rose. I do believe she is engaged to be married to a Mr. Rice, but perhaps I will win her heart before she takes that dreadful step. I do not think so; Mr. Rice is a delightful gentleman, and Miss Pruyn seems positively smitten. In truth I am half cracked about this young lady, but I fear she does not return the feeling. Please write me soon. I am anxious to hear all the news from home, although it is not my home any longer.

Your affectionate and loving friend,
Julia T. Martin

*   *   *   *

Years later when I looked again at the photographs of Julia, Julie, and I dressed as men, I wondered about what we all had in mind as we chose those outfits. Of course we did it for a lark, but I do think it was also an expression of how pretentious men can be, and how we could be as good as or better than men. Not that we had any desire to be men—none of us did. It was rather that we did not need men in our lives. A woman could be a devoted lover to another woman, as Gertrude and I were to one another. And Julia and I certainly knew from experience that a gentleman could upset a young woman's life in a myriad of ways. In any event, none of us especially enjoyed male companionship. Life seemed jollier without it. I must smile to myself when I think of that photograph; it seemed as though dressing in costume was a joke with no serious significance, but as with the photograph of Trude and me in slips and masks, when we dressed in different clothing, we could almost be different people. We were no longer *ladies*. We could be anyone we wanted to be and say almost anything we wanted. We could speak with our outfits, as it were. Sometimes I think that we were barely aware of what we were thinking when we chose our costumes and poses, but like a writer who chooses one particular word over another to suggest something beyond the obvious, we were trying to say something that was not talked about in our set. As that queer poet Emily Dickinson said in her poetry, "tell the truth / but tell it slant."

*   *   *   *

In the summer of 1892, I traveled to Bennington to visit Julia and her friend Mrs. Snively. During the first three weeks of this vacation, Julia, Mrs. Snively, and her two sons were devoted guides, showing me as much of the Vermont countryside as they could. We traveled to Williamstown in Massachusetts so that I might see Williams College. We saw monuments, streams, mountains, falls, and some lovely covered bridges. Everywhere we went, I took my camera, a task made easier with the assistance of Mrs. Snively's two young sons, who assisted with the trunk. And I tried to photograph everything I saw. The landscape was truly magnificent. But in the last week, when we remained in Bennington itself, I turned my camera to my friends.

I had great admiration for Julia, who had had to make a new life for herself after having grown up in circumstances of relative ease, and I had a similar high regard for Mrs. Snively. Mrs. Snively had been married to a minister in Albany, New York. The Reverend Mr. Snively was well respected in the community, so that when Mrs. Snively filed for divorce from him on the grounds of cruelty, the city as a whole was aghast and immediately jumped to Mr. Snively's defense. I know that divorce is accepted in this day and age, but back in the 1880s, when Mrs. Snively filed for hers, it was not only unusual, it was also disgraceful. It was common among lower-class women to flit from one man to the next, but not among women of our status. And not only did Mrs. Snively ask to dissolve her marriage, but she demanded custody of her boys on the grounds that Mr. Snively was cruel to them as well as to his wife.

When the news of the divorce became public, the sentiment largely favored Mr. Snively, with most people believing that Mrs. Snively had either lost her sanity or was having an affair, or both. However, as the case progressed through the courts, Mrs. Snively was able to convince the presiding judge and the majority of the public that Mr. Snively, while presenting a benign demeanor in public, was a terror within his own home. Quite remarkably the judge decided in Mrs. Snively's favor, granting her the divorce and custody of her two sons. While her former husband remained in Albany for a time, Mrs. Snively moved to Bennington, taking the boys and her own mother, the frail Mrs. Cooper. Incidentally Mr. Snively never recovered from the scandal, moving from one town to the next in search of a congregation that would have him.

For all the difficulties that Mrs. Snively had been through, one would expect her to have a somewhat dour personality. This was far from the case, and while I had enjoyed traveling about the countryside, the real joy of this trip was to be found when we settled in at Mrs. Snively's for a week. She was certainly a woman who knew how to enjoy herself. I shall never forget our trip to the county fair, near Bennington, when we posed behind one of those painted displays with holes through which we could poke our heads. Mrs. Snively had insisted that because I was such a strong and hearty girl, I should pose as the gentleman with the lady's handbag. We dubbed ourselves the Simpkins family. It is interesting that in later years, after I acquired a Franklin motorcar, I did carry a handbag about with me, but unlike the other ladies, mine was filled with tools that I could use to make minor repairs on the car. I suppose in some ways, I was perhaps a man with a handbag. Although, Lord knows, I would never have enjoyed being a man.

But those days in Vermont were wonderful. Mrs. Snively had a companion by then, Mary Sanford, and they were so joyful that one could not help but smile and laugh in their presence. I recall taking a photograph of the two of them dancing a jig with their ankles showing. All these years later, I am still touched by the beauty of their happiness at that moment.

On my last night with Julia before my scheduled return home, Julia, Mrs. Snively, and I climbed into bed together for one last photograph. There was a part of me that wished that I could remain where I was in that picture, between the warmth of Julia and her friend Mrs. Snively. When we parted company, I promised to visit again, but I never did. My life and Julia's diverged in so many ways that we rarely saw each other again. We only did when she came to Staten Island to see her mother, who sometimes lived in a leased house and was sometimes confined to a hospital. But Julia and I continued to write each other for several more years.

Julia remained in Vermont, and because of her father's losses, she found it necessary to earn an income of her own. Julia's education had trained her for very little that would be lucrative, but through the kindness of Mrs. Snively, she gained employment as a companion to Mrs. Cooper, Mrs. Snively's mother. At first Julia was pleased with that position, but over time she came to realize that Mrs. Cooper was not only frail, but also cranky and very demanding.

August 23, 1892
Julia Martin
c/o Mrs. Cooper
Bennington, Vermont

My dear Alice,

Saturday night finds me sitting at Mrs. Cooper's dining-room table, waiting for Mrs. Thompson, our neighbor, and Mrs. Cooper to get through playing backgammon, and I think I cannot do better than have a chat on paper with you. There are a few exciting moments here, but it is often a struggle to find them. Your letters to me, therefore, are a relief from my daily routine. As I wrote you previously, Miss Hattie Pruyn is now Mrs. Rice, and she is currently in Europe on an extended wedding trip. While I am happy for Hattie, I do feel sorrow for myself, because she was perhaps my most interesting companion for so many months.

You will, I think, remember Miss Wellington from your summer visit two years ago. Well, she came in and asked me to play tennis with her and some of the other girls this afternoon. Mrs. Cooper was not inclined to have me go—for no reason, as Mrs. Thompson and Mrs. Metcalf are here to keep Mrs. Cooper company. I was rather out of sorts most of the day, particularly as it had been Mrs. Cooper herself who suggested that Miss Wellington invite me. Mrs. Cooper had me read aloud to her for two hours from two until four in the afternoon. At four thirty, Mrs. Cooper announced that she and her friends would be going out for an afternoon drive, and she said that I could now go to Miss Wellington's. Miss Wellington and I played doubles against Mr. King and his wife. You will remember that he is tall and slim, and she is short and fat. In attempting to reach a ball that was hit almost directly to her, Mrs. King somehow tripped Mr. King, who tumbled and sprained his ankle. And that was the end of our game.

On Tuesday and Wednesday I will be visiting in Albany with Mr. and Mrs. McHarg. I want to buy a lot of things for the winter dressmaking. Dear me, I hardly know myself. After a year in service to Mrs. Cooper, I have become quite domestic. I have also learned to stand up for myself. I think I told you about Mrs. Cooper's guest, Lady Hillhouse, a woman who clearly looked down on me as though I were a lesser being. She is to return again on the thirty-first, and I have decided that should she behave in a condescending manner toward me this time…well, let her try that false sweetness on me, and she will notice a strong reaction from this quarter.

Mrs. Snively, Miss Sanford, and the boys are still away. I miss them all so much. I have grown quite fond of Mrs. Snively. Since Mrs. Snively is away, I drive her horse and buggy to all of Mrs. Cooper's errands in the village, and so on. It has been great fun in spite of the fact that Mrs. Cooper insists that someone accompany me. Nevertheless it is wonderful to ride through the country, away from the demands of Mrs. Cooper. I do appreciate that she has taken me on, but sometimes I do feel sorry for myself and miss my old life.

I hope I shall have the chance to visit with you on the island this fall, or that you will be able to come to stay with me. I am impatient to see you again, but I will make an effort to exert my patience a little longer. How is your dear family? Please send my regards to one and all.

Now good-bye with best love, believe me,
Affectionately,
Julia T. Martin

*   *   *   *

Julia stayed on as Mrs. Cooper's companion for slightly less than two years, and their time together did not improve Julia's opinion of Mrs. Cooper. One of the reasons I never saw Julia again was that Mrs. Cooper did not want Julia to have her own friends in the house or to have anything about that might distract Julia from her "duties." Those duties were essentially composed of catering to whatever whim Mrs. Cooper had at any given moment. Poor Julia.

13 May 1893
Julia Martin
c/o Mrs. Cooper
Bennington, Vermont

Dear Alice,

I do hope this letter reaches you before you leave the Richards' home. Your adventures in Concord, Massachusetts, must have kept you very busy, as I have received only one letter from you. *But* I was so glad to receive that last letter. You are always so good and kind to me. Would it not be a lark if we could meet before you go home? But I have been making inquiries and to come here takes you way out of your way. If Mrs. Snively were here, I know she would ask you to stay with her. Do you remember the fun we had when we stayed with Mrs. Snively last summer? If Mrs. Cooper were not such a pig, begging her pardon, she would ask you, if only for one night. There is no one here now, and there is no one for a week. After that her house is to be full of her own friends—and it would give me such a pleasure to see you.

It hardly pays for me to come to Staten Island, as Mrs. Cooper only grants me ten days, and so much of that time would be taken up visiting with Mama, who, as you know, is somewhat unsettled in her new surroundings. I do not think it best to ask Mrs. Cooper for a longer vacation, as I will have to hear her tell me how generous she already has been with me.

You know, Alice, on no account must you in any way hint at anything that I write you. I trust you in writing, and I think it better for you to tear my letters. If I ever left Mrs. Cooper, it should be on the plea of beginning something that would be my life work, which would be true. I feel that if I live with Mrs. Cooper for five years, and then she dies, and I am thirty years old, I should be able to begin something new. However, if I stay too long, it will be too late for me.

Now enough about myself. Bennington in spring looks as marvelous as usual, and my life though pleasant is sometimes tiresome. I look up at our room at Mrs. Snively's from time to time and think. I am glad we were together that summer.

In love and affection always,
Julia T. Martin

*   *   *   *

Julia had thought she would stay with Mrs. Cooper for five years. I don't know how she thought that, as the woman was truly impossible to deal with—she would summon or dismiss Julia on a whim so often that Julia never truly had time for herself. As it turned out, Mrs. Snively tired of the cold New England winters, and in the late spring of 1893, she and Mrs. Cooper traveled to California to seek a better climate, leaving Julia in the lurch with no means of support. But Julia was never one to stay down long, and she managed to secure herself a position at the St. Agnes School in Schenectady, New York.

22 November 1893
Julia Martin
c/o St. Agnes School
Schenectady

Dear Alice,

I have just come from church and before even turning around, I intend to send you a letter.

Mrs. Cooper, Mrs. Snively, and the children are gone thousands of miles away, and I am left, in one way feeling desolate enough and in others too joyful to live. At the last (three days before Mrs. Cooper started out), she begged me to go, and for Mrs. Snively's sake, I came very near to yielding, but in every way felt it would be most unwise to go. Mrs. Cooper found someone else to accompany her. In the months that I tended to Mrs. Cooper, I have grown, without being conscious of it, so dependent and so very fond of Mrs. Snively that when I felt she was going from me, I was very much broken up. She has been such a good and true friend of mine, and I would have enjoyed being with her this winter, but I was reluctant to travel so far from my other friends. I would be even more dependent on Mrs. Snively and more responsible for Mrs. Cooper and consequently felt that I would feel terribly confined.

I was promised a position at the St. Agnes School, and I felt it was an opportunity that was too good to lose. I am working here now, and I live at the school. If Mrs. Cooper returns next summer, I shall live with her again, although she is getting old and is very selfish and expects more of me than I can give her. I do think living with Mrs. Cooper is a very unhealthy life for me at this time. With Mrs. Cooper, even my idle time did not feel as though it were my own. Here at St. Agnes School, a feeling of rest has come over me that you cannot imagine.

On my next holiday, Mr. McHarg and his family have asked me to accompany them to the World's Fair in Chicago. We are going on the same excursion train, and it is costing $16, which will leave me busted for the rest of my life. Am I not a fool? Do not tell this to your family; I fear they will believe I am not in my sane mind.

Lovingly,
Julia T. Martin

May 7, 1894
Julia Martin
Albany, New York

Dearest Alice,

I was indeed very sorry to hear of your grandfather's death and yet felt glad that the old man passed away so quietly and has not longer to linger on. Life to me is our great mystery of uncertainty. One minute we are here; the next we are away.

I feel this because my life is so varied. What do you think now that I expect to go to Santa Barbara, probably next week, for the whole summer? I found a telegram awaiting my arrival from Schenectady on Friday morning asking if I would come "expense paid, terms as before." This was the first that I knew that Mrs. Snively and Mrs. Cooper would not be coming east for the summer. Am I glad? Yes, very. The trip will be delightful, and it is always an education to go to new places, and of course I am glad to see Mrs. Snively. But Alice, I feel it is a very long way to go all alone away from my friends and the few who are very dear to me, and somehow I feel that it will be longer than the summer. I feel that it is the best thing to do for lots and lots of reasons, and I am wild with delight and blue as blue can be, if you can understand my mixture of feelings. I shall write Mama today about my plans. I did think I would be able to come down for a visit, but find that it is impossible. I will write next Sunday and tell you when I start, etc., etc.

Love to all,
Affectionately,
Julia T. Martin

*   *   *   *

I do wonder what became of Julia. She left for California, full of hope for the future, and I must admit it was no surprise to me that someone as spirited and independent as Julia finally found a sufficient means of support. She took it upon herself to start a boardinghouse in Santa Barbara, and she seemed to be making a success of it. She was quite excited by her new business venture and full of plans for the future. Julia invited me and Mama to come out and stay with her, but we never did. The last I heard of Julia was several years later, when she almost had a burst appendix and required emergency surgery.

Eleanor E. Colman
Santa Barbara, California
March 4, 1898

Dear Miss Austen,

Miss Julia Martin wishes me to write to you telling you of her illness. She was so dreadfully weak that I did not dare to ask her how much you knew of her bout with appendicitis and her subsequent operation. Julia has been living and keeping up in willpower. Of course you do know how great a success she has made of her house, making it a home in every sense for all of us wanderers. I have lived at Miss Martin's house for well over two years in spite of the fact that when I arrived I thought to spend only a month.

About last September, I believe, she had the first attack, which sent her to the hospital. After three or four subsequent attacks, her physician bundled her over to the hospital again, where she had another attack that was really dreadful. She was operated on, and it turned out to be just in time, as her appendix was in danger of bursting. Poor Julia was so brave and so utterly alone way out here, but she has made some good friends here too.

Julia keeps your pictures on the mantel in the parlor, so your face, in its many incarnations, is familiar to me, and of course, Julia speaks of you often, so that I feel that we are not strangers.

Yours truly,
Miss Eleanor E. Colman

Western Union Telegram to:
Miss Eleanor E. Colman
c/o Julia Martin
1624 Garden Street
Santa Barbara, California
From: Miss Alice Austen
Rosebank, Staten Island

Letter received *stop* please keep posted of progress *stop* give love, anxious, thanks *stop* Alice Austen *STOP*

*   *   *   *

Miss Colman kept me up to date on Julia's condition for a time, but the physical distance between Julia and me was so great that, although I will always feel close to Julia, our friendship could not be sustained. Miss Colman's letter telling me that Julia was on the mend was the last word I heard about Julia. It saddens me to think about losing contact with her, because I feel that in so many ways, she was an inspiration to me. She was the first girl with whom I became friendly who was willing to live a life at odds with what was expected—and who made a success of it. Until that point, I had never given much thought to my own future, expecting somehow that someday I would live according to the conventions of society. Julia showed me a different way.

Chapter Six

Julia was not the only girl I knew who had no interest in marrying and who had crushes on other women. When I was a student at the Miss Errington School, I became friendly with Carrie and Violet Ward. They were unmarried sisters who lived together their entire lives in their father's beautiful mansion. Through Vi and Carrie, I met Daisy Elliott, a woman whom I would classify as bohemian and who ran a gymnasium for young ladies in New York, the Berkeley Athletic Club.

Daisy was one of the foremost proponents of the positive value of physical exercise for women. When Grandmother and Mama were girls, physical exercise had often been viewed as harmful to a female body, but physicians have come to realize that with some restrictions, girls can benefit from healthy outdoor activities such as tennis and bicycling. Physicians have also discovered the benefits of indoor exercise for women, such as stretching, especially for women who suffer from nervous disorders. Where once a doctor might recommend bed rest and quiet for a young neurasthenic lady, a few of today's modernized physicians would prescribe mild exercise to promote recovery and regular exercise with India clubs and on rings in the gym to maintain good health. And of course, as one recovered one's health, a modern physician would, in addition, advocate some outdoor activity such as walking or cycling.

Daisy Elliott was an early proponent of this course of treatment, and as it has become more popular and medically accepted, Daisy has made quite a financial success of her gymnasium in Manhattan, treating both patients and healthy women who seek to engage in physical exercise. However, while Daisy's professional life was quite accomplished, she was dealing with understanding her feelings about women and "against" men, as she described it—just like me. We had many, many serious discussions on the topic, and these talks helped her understand her feelings, especially the deep love she felt for Carrie Ward. As a result of this sharing of opinions, Daisy and I developed a strong and devoted friendship—one that was a source of comfort for both of us.

---

14 February 1897
Daisy Elliott
77 Park Avenue
New York, New York

My dearest love, Alice,

I am sending you this valentine. I must apologize for want of originality in my selection, but I believe that you will take it in the spirit in which I send it. Ever since I have had mine from you, I have felt that you ought to have one too, and naturally I prefer you have it from me.

You know that I love you, darling; there are many things I think of that I would like to do for you, yet there is so little I really can. Whenever there is anything I could do and don't, please let me know, because there is nothing that gives me more true pleasure than doing for one as I love as much as you. You have brought me so much happiness at a time when I could see nothing but misery, that nothing I can ever do for you will ever equal it. I would like you to find as much happiness as I have begun to find with my dear Carrie—sometime I believe you will darling.

Always faithfully yours,
Daisy

*   *   *   *

Daisy was an avid bicyclist and encouraged Vi, Carrie, and myself to participate as well. In the summer of 1897, Daisy had asked me to join her and Carrie on a bicycle tour of Europe, an invitation that I had declined, as I had committed myself to visit Trude at Twilight Rest that summer. I was sorry to have missed the opportunity for such an adventure. But I did meet Gertrude that summer, which was more than adequate compensation for having missed a bicycle adventure in Europe.

25 July 1897
Daisy Elliott
Salzburg, Austria

Alice dear,

At last a letter from you! I knew I wanted it very much, but didn't realize how much until it was really here. It is funny too—it had the same effect that being with you has; you know how quieting that is. It is nice to feel that this connecting thread stretches across the ocean in both directions, from you to me as well as from me to you. I really have been pretty homesick, and your letter has given me a new start.

In the autumn, when I return, we can have some more good rides together. I look forward to that time with great anticipation. How lovely that your bicycle is a '97! Does it coast well? How goes the brown saddle? Mine is very satisfactory. The other day, we were caught in a hard rain and sought refuge in a peasant's cottage for an hour, but ventured out too soon and got drenched and covered with mud. Sent my dress to the tailors, and it came out like new; it took me an age to clean my wheel—I took off the chain guard to get the chain. I hate that guard and am sorry my dress is not short enough to dispense with it. Have you one on? People couldn't stare at us more if I were wearing only my blue checked knickerbockers, so perhaps Carrie and I should feel free to wear bloomers after all. It would surely add to our adventures, and would save my dresses from the mud and dirt. The temptation is great. In the fall, perhaps you and the other girls will join me in starting a new bicycling fashion.

I shall write again soon. Please write me also.

All my love and affection,
Daisy

August 27, 1897
Daisy Elliot
Bretagne, France

My dear Alice,

It is a beautiful afternoon, and as I sit here at my window overlooking the pretty town and bay, it seems almost as if I had gone back to Italy and was looking over the Bay of Naples. It is very beautiful, and I have enjoyed this adventure so much. However, my thoughts have been way over the water today, even more than usual. Perhaps your letter and the one from Violet, which came together last night, have taken possession of me for certainly I feel longings both to remain in Europe and to come home in order to straighten out the problems that have developed between you two.

Carrie and I have had so many adventures over the past two months. We have cycled through the Alps for miles and miles; we have met a wide array of people from all over the world, it seems, and we have seen the most fantastic scenery. I wish that we were as adept as you with the camera, so that we would have been able to record the passing scene. It is locked in my memory, but I wish that it could be shared more readily. You are so lucky, dear Alice, to have the talent that you have. I was thinking this morning of the old peasant couple that sheltered us in the rain a few weeks ago, and how wonderful it would be to have a picture of their faces, which were filled with lines and the wisdom of the ages. Ah, but alas, I have no such talent, so you will have to rely on my stories and Carrie's if you are to share this experience with us. I wish that you could have come, although, as you said in your last letter, it is good that you did not. Your Gertrude sounds like a true find and as rare as a precious stone. Alice, sometimes it is hard to believe your luck—a talent for both photography and for uncovering beautiful souls.

As for me, I have enjoyed this adventure and have seen so many startling things. In Bretagne, I have not much chance to see bicyclers here, but the few I have seen wear *pants*! See, perhaps this will become the fashion among women bicyclers on the island.

This letter is very dull and hardly worth sending; but it does take my love to *you*, which to me is something. A month from today, I shall be sailing toward home.

Yours in love always,
Daisy

Violet Ward
77 Park Avenue
New York, New York
February 21, 1895

Dearest Alice,

How your ears must be ringing, dear one. Daisy, Carrie, and I have been up half the night talking and planning a book that Daisy and I have agreed to write for Brentano's. Perhaps we have already mentioned it? It is to be a bicycling guide for ladies, instructing them on how to ride—proper position, proper clothing, and that sort of thing. The publisher has told us that pictures would be a great help to the gentleman who is to prepare the woodcuts, and naturally we thought of you. Daisy and Carrie have agreed to pose on the bicycle if you will snap the pictures. What do you think, old girl? Is it to your liking?

I will be home in a few days and perhaps we can arrange for the four of us to talk and make plans. I do hope this cold weather finds you warm and cozy.

Love with affection,
Violet Ward

*   *   *   *

A year or so before Daisy left on her European jaunt with Carrie, Vi contacted me concerning a book she was preparing with Daisy, called *Bicycling for Ladies*. The publisher, Brentano, suggested that illustrations would be appropriate, and that photographs would be required on which to model the woodcut pictures. Vi of course thought of me, dear friend that she is. We had such a wonderful time posing Daisy on her bicycle in correct and incorrect postures. It was my first time dealing with backdrops and studio work. It was really the only time that I did that sort of thing.

I know that by the 1890s, many girls were setting up their own studios and were working as professional photographers. I was aware of women who worked for hire, such as Frances Benjamin Johnston of Washington DC. How could I not be aware of Miss Johnston? Her photographs of the colored people of the Hampton Institute, a training school for freed slaves and children of freed slaves, were quite well-known and considered remarkable, as were her portraits of famous Americans. Her articles on technique and business practices were in all the popular ladies' magazines, and she seemed to have achieved some sort of status as the center for the women in the world of professional photography. I did read her articles with interest in the *Ladies' Home Journal,* and I was a member of a camera club with some other girls, so I did keep up on the latest in the world of photography and photographers.

I loved to exchange ideas about photography and equipment with other people. Even as an older woman, I was happy to engage in talk about such things. Gertrude's brother-in-law and her young nephew Tate and I were exchanging ideas on photography as late as the 1940s, when I could rarely afford to take pictures. Photography was my first love, I suppose, before even Gertrude, but unlike the followers of Miss Johnston and unlike the other ladies in my camera club, I had no interest in setting up a studio and making one portrait after the other. Nor did I feel it was appropriate for a lady to accept remuneration for any work. I know that many girls did, but I did not want to give the appearance that my grandfather was unable to support me. Although I admired the independent spirit that Julia Martin showed in starting her boardinghouse, there was something disgraceful in her having had to grub for money to support herself. It reflected negatively on her father, and I did not want to do the same to my family.

But at the same time, I became fascinated with portraiture. I made portraits of my friends and their husbands and children, and I did photograph my family often, but not in a studio. I preferred to take pictures in a natural setting—the outdoors, a person's home, and so on. I have always believed that the best way to capture a person's true essence—which is what photographic portraiture, in my experience, was supposed to concern itself with—is to utilize natural surroundings. And I liked my pictures to have a direct quality about them.

*   *   *   *

Mr. Oglesby is visiting again. I have enjoyed his little visits over the last few months; they make the time in this miserable poorhouse go a bit faster. This time he asks me about several pictures, and many of them are of my home. I must have photographed that house from every angle and in every season. It wasn't simply that I thought that our home was beautiful, which it certainly was, and that I wanted a pictorial record of it. Rather I took pictures of it over and over again because of what it meant to me. It was my safe harbor and the center of my world. When I think of my childhood, I remember the warmth and the comfort that I found there from my family and from the very air inside. I loved to come home to Clear Comfort in all seasons. In the hot months, there were the cooling breezes that traveled across the terrace from the bay and through the long piazza windows. In the colder months, it was a warm retreat from the icy winds that blew off the same water. In the evenings, Mama and I would sit by the fire with Uncle Pete, Papa, and Grandmother, each of us engaged quietly in our own occupation—reading, needlework, or study—and none of us felt alone.

When I first began taking pictures, they were mostly taken at our home; many of them were of the ships that passed our terrace. No ship could enter or leave New York without sailing by Clear Comfort, and I did love the majestic sight of the boats as they sailed by. I also photographed members of my family and friends, usually on the terrace or the piazza. (I was not too fond of using a flash indoors, because the ignited powder that created the flash could cause serious burns, although I never burned myself.) My pug dog, Punch, was also a favored subject for me. I loved to pose him, and he always cooperated.

As I think back on these early pictures now, and try to imagine what I was thinking when I chose my subjects, I recall that my main objective was to capture images of the people and things I loved and who were a part of my life. I am quite taken with the idea that I could stop something I loved long enough to record it on a glass plate that I could keep for all time—or so I thought when I was young. So when I was at our home and, later, when I traveled on my summer vacations, I carried my camera and recorded my family, friends, and the beauty of nature.

*   *   *   *

I think some of my most interesting photographs were the ones I took on my travels. I was always ready to see new places and new things, and so whenever the opportunity to seek an adventure presented itself, I jumped at the opportunity. In 1893 I traveled to the Chicago World's Fair, the Columbian Exposition, which honored the four hundredth anniversary of Columbus's discovery of the New World. It was such an exciting trip, and I made a commitment to myself to photograph every step of the journey. I remember that it was the first of July when I started out, and since it was to be such a distance from home, the good-byes were long and lingering. I photographed myself as I prepared to part on my journey with Punch, the dog. It was a humorous picture, in my mind—I was attempting to replicate the typical man and his wife preparing to begin a long journey. Punch played the role of my "wife," seated in a chair, which I stood beside, while holding his paw in my hand. I carried the usual accoutrements associated with a gentleman—a large umbrella and a leather traveling case. It came off quite well, although it was perhaps too subtle for most people outside of my immediate family to understand.

I traveled west by train, of course, and took several photographs of the scenery I passed en route. I was glued to my window, because I had never traveled in this direction before, and everything seemed so exotic. But the fair itself was truly wondrous and fascinating, and I spent most of every day that I was there photographing some aspect of it. The architecture was spectacular, and it was hard to believe that it had been constructed of temporary materials in such a short span of time. It looked so permanent and so carefully built. I was fascinated with the new technology that was everywhere—especially the electric fountain, the Ferris wheel, and the exhibits of new modes of transportation on display in the Transportation Building. For some reason, the exhibit in the California Hall of the Liberty Bell constructed out of oranges stays in my mind.

I must have taken a hundred photographs in the two weeks I was in Chicago. This may not seem like so much to someone who uses celluloid roll film in one of those new little cameras, but it was quite an accomplishment for someone working with glass plates and a large, old-fashioned machine. I was very proud of those photographs.

13 July 1893
Alice Austen
University of Chicago
Chicago, Illinois

Dear Julia,

I cannot tell you how wonderful the fair here has been, and I do hope you will have the opportunity to pay a visit. It is a true marvel and spectacle. On the first day at the fair, we went straightaway to see the Ferris wheel. And of course we took our turn on it. I wished I could have photographed the fair from the height of the wheel, but of course, with my bulky camera, that was not possible.

Over the next several days, we explored the various exhibitions. The electric fountain is simply marvelous at night. But the aspect of the fair that has captured my imagination has been the architecture. The fairgrounds can be navigated by gondola along canals that simulate Venice. The buildings have been constructed in the Greek style and have a look of permanence about them, and yet I am told that the entire fair is only semipermanent, almost like plaster of paris. I could see how fragile it all was when a fire broke out in a cold-storage building the other day. The building simply disintegrated.

What have I seen? I have seen and photographed everything from the parades of the Columbian guards to the caravels. I visited the houses of the various states and was especially intrigued by the western states' exhibitions, with their Indians and their totem poles. I have made more than one visit to the Arts Building, and I have taken countless pictures of all the buildings' exteriors. I have taken several experimental photographs of the water fountains to see if I can capture their grace.

I have also seen a little of Chicago itself, and it was nice, but not as interesting to me as New York or New England. Tomorrow we leave to head back east. I will be home for a short visit and then I will be off to Mauch Chunk, Pennsylvania, and later in August off to Lake George to visit with Bessie Watrous and her family at Camp Inn, which is directly on the lake. I shall not return home until the end of September, so as you can see, my plate this summer is quite full.

I do miss you, Julia. You are so important to me, and I love you dearly. I do hope that you will be able to take an extended trip to the island to visit with us and see your mother. We had such a lovely time last August, and I would like to duplicate it sometime in the not-too-distant future. I hope that this letter finds you well and relatively at peace. I know that your situation is a difficult one, and I want to remind you that I would help you in any way that I could.

Yours lovingly,
Alice

*   *   *   *

Years later, in 1901, I attended the World's Fair in Buffalo, New York, and although that fair received considerably less attention than the one in Chicago, I enjoyed visiting there as well and photographed it just as avidly. At the Buffalo fair, I was particularly attracted to the midway because of the effort that was made to put on display people and items from distant cultures. Aunt Minn and Uncle Oswald's talk of all the places they visited had sparked my interest in other peoples, and the Buffalo fair was the first and only time I was able to see them.

8 August 1901
Alice Austen
Buffalo, New York

Dear Aunt Minn,

What an exhausting and exhilarating World's Fair this is, with countries represented from around the world—the Philippines, Japan, Spain, Egypt, Mexico, and so on. This truly is a fair that celebrates the world. And the construction is marvelous; it is like a planned city. Gertrude and I think that this will be a model for cities to come. Everything is laid out so sensibly, and the landscape design is a marvel of greenery and waterways. It is like the fair of 1893 in that one can travel from one section to another by boat, and yet it is much grander. The individual countries have constructed whole villages to show how their peoples' lives are. There is even a Darkest Africa section that is so frightening and exotic. And of course the various countries' "villages" are peopled by natives in their traditional costumes or clothing, making one feel as though one has traveled across the globe.

Yesterday Gertrude and I witnessed a bullfight in the Mexican tradition. Today we saw the parade on the midway, which featured animals and people from all the countries represented here. We were most impressed with the elephants' procession and the trained bears.

I have taken well over one hundred photographs so far. That is how determined I am to capture every detail. The most remarkable feature of the fair is the nighttime illumination of many of the buildings. It is so bright that I have been able to take several night photographs of the illuminated structures. I do hope these have been successful. But if they have not been, I have carefully tried to picture every aspect of this fair. It is such a marvel, and I am sure it will be talked about in years to come.

I will be home by the end of next week, and I look forward to spending some time with you, Aunt Minn. Are the dogs and cats well taken care of? I do so worry about my little children. Gertrude sends her love.

Lovingly,
Loll

*   *   *   *

Actually I am one of the few people I know who even remember that there was a World's Fair in Buffalo. Those who do recall the fair remember it only because President McKinley was shot there and later died of his wounds.

In the autumn preceding my trip to Chicago—that would be the fall of 1892—I took another interesting extended trip. My Aunt Nellie—my aunt by marriage to my Uncle Pete—and her father, Ralph Munroe, loved to sail as much as I did. They both invited me to join them on an extended sailing trip down the eastern coast of the United States. He was sailing to Coconut Grove in southern Florida, where he owned a home and was developing real estate in anticipation of a boom in South Florida. Mr. Munroe's boat, the *Wabun*, was berthed in New Brunswick, which is where Aunt Nellie, Uncle Pete, and Mr. Munroe, whom I nicknamed Butterball because of his generous girth, began our trip. We sailed south through inland waterways and canals all the way to Washington DC. It took us slightly more than two weeks, and it was truly an adventure sailing down the Delaware River to Annapolis and the Naval Academy. I saw a side of life I had not seen on Staten Island. I was struck by the way people lived along the river, and I became fascinated by the lives of darkies who depended on the water of the Chesapeake Bay for their livelihood.

October 28, 1892
Alice Austen
Washington DC

Dearest Julia,

How exciting this trip has been! Uncle Pete, Aunt Nellie, and Mr. Munroe, Uncle Pete's father-in-law (whom I call Butterball) are excellent traveling companions. It is a good thing too, as the cockpit and cabin of our little sailing ship, *Wabun*, are very small, and we are constantly in close contact. From the very first day when we set off on the Raritan River Canal from Uncle Pete's home in New Brunswick, New Jersey, to the day we arrived here in the nation's capital, I have enjoyed every moment. After we left the Raritan River Canal at Trenton, we went on to Philadelphia, which is a beautiful and interesting city. I saw a beautiful four-masted schooner as we sailed the *Wabun* into the harbor at Philadelphia. As I have done with every interesting aspect of this trip, I took a picture.

I am fascinated by the mechanics of this trip—how the mules pull the boats through the canals, so we do not have to depend on good winds, and how the locks raise and lower the boats from one water level to the other. After we left the Raritan Canal, we traveled through the Delaware River Canal to the Chesapeake Bay, passing close to settlements along the river. There are many darkies who make their living from the Delaware River and the Chesapeake. Along the Chesapeake Bay, we passed some living on a heap of shells from shucked oysters. It was as large as a small hill. We stopped along the way to watch the Negroes shuck the shells that later became their small homestead.

Finally we arrived at Annapolis, where we disembarked. Over the last several days, Nellie and I have seen many fascinating sights. We visited the State House at Annapolis and the Naval Academy, then went on to Washington. What a thrill it was to stand before the White House and to visit the Capitol Building. How majestic it all looks! We have arrived in time to see Mrs. Harrison's splendid funeral procession from the White House. I have taken so many pictures along the canals and in Washington, I shall be busy the entire winter printing the good ones.

I am ready now to return home, although it would be quite exciting to sail on to southern Florida with Butterball. Coconut Grove, where he has built a home, sounds quite exotic, and I would love to see the surrounding jungles and perhaps even see a passing panther. Butterball says that someday a railroad will probably be constructed through the jungle connecting Jacksonville, Florida, to the southern reaches of that state, and then we shall all be able to travel easily to Butterball's home. With the railroads growing at a remarkable rate, I do think he is right. But at the moment, it is only reached by boat, and the next leg of Butterball's journey through the great dismal swamp does sound arduous. So I shall be on my way home in a few days and shall certainly arrive well before the Hunt Breakfast at the Wiman Farm House on Staten Island on Election Day.

I do miss you, dearest Julia, and hope that I shall see you soon. Will you be coming to the island this fall?

Lovingly yours,
Alice

*   *   *   *

I thoroughly enjoyed these extended trips and the opportunity they afforded to see and photograph different locations, but when I came back to Clear Comfort from the summer of 1893, I began to feel somewhat dissatisfied with my photography. I thought the images were beautifully composed and lit, and I was proud of the record I had created, but something was lacking, and I was looking for it. In the winter of the year following the Chicago trip, I stayed at home and spent a great deal of time photographing painted portraits and artifacts in the house, and when the weather brightened a bit, I found I was anxious to get away to do something new. I was not sure what it would be, but I took my camera to New York and photographed people who worked in the open air, selling goods and offering entertainment.

Mr. Oglesby has asked me to tell him about my motivation for taking pictures of immigrants and working-class people. I think that perhaps he thought I had some ulterior motive like those do-good ladies of my generation who were opening settlement houses to aid the poor. But the truth was that this project appealed to me, especially after my sailing trip with Mr. Munroe, during which I had seen how many of the poorer people along the rivers and waterways lived. I had done a considerable amount of traveling and become curious about the working classes and the poor in New York. How did they live? What did they look like when they were in their natural surroundings?

On my first photographic trip to New York, I told Mr. Oglesby, I had been filled with a great deal of trepidation, so I began rather tentatively by simply pointing my camera, from some distance, at people as they worked. As a lady of the upper classes, I was unaccustomed to wandering the streets of working-class neighborhoods. People of my status generally associated with the laboring classes and tradespeople only when there was business to conduct, and I had to admit that a part of me was rather fearful of them and their neighborhood. They were not simply people from foreign places—everything about them was foreign. Their manners were different from mine, and their standards of behavior were certainly lower. Their homes were one on top of the other, so they lived their lives in each other's laps, seeming to place little value on the appearance of virtue or privacy.

I had read about women with backgrounds similar to mine who were going into the tenement neighborhoods in order to establish settlement houses where new immigrants and members of the lower classes could learn how to take care of themselves and their families like proper Americans, but I never had any interest in such a project. As far as I could see from my travels among these people, the settlement houses, while admirable in their goals, had done little in the direction of improving these people's lives. I knew that some photographers were participating in the crusade to improve the lot of the working classes by documenting the dismal conditions of their homes and workplaces, but I shall make it clear to Mr. Oglesby that I had no such project in mind. I was simply looking for something new and different to photograph.

I was reluctant to set foot into the poorest neighborhoods; they really were quite dangerous in those days. Sometimes even the police were reluctant to enter the tenement areas for fear of being set upon. So I sought the working class out in the business neighborhoods. I took my camera to New York's main shopping district, along Sixth Avenue. This is where ladies did all their shopping, and where the best dry goods and large stores were. Under the El—the elevated train—there were men and women hawking their wares and services. These people were marvelous subjects for my camera. I remember a man grinding knives, another selling shoestring, a crippled boy selling newspapers, and a man and woman making music with a small piano and tambourine. I became a little braver as the day progressed; I went east a few blocks and took several pictures of bootblacks at their stand.

On a second photographic expedition to New York, I stayed near South Street, an area that I was fairly familiar with, as it was the location of the ferry landing. The fish market at Fulton Street caught my attention—there was so much frenetic activity, and it was all so new to me. The European immigrants were selling fish and sponges; there were colored people there too, as there had been on the river near Annapolis. The Negroes did a variety of things, such as cleaning the surrounding streets, which were always slippery with fish entrails, and the darkies also chopped the ice that was used to preserve the fish. It was all very exciting to me, and the people seemed quite happy—and maybe a little bit stunned—to have a lady's camera pointed at them as they worked.

I went back to the East Side, to the immigrant neighborhoods, about a week later and visited an outdoor market on Hester Street, where eggs and cake and bread were being sold and bought by immigrant women. I was fascinated by them—their lives seemed to me to be so hard, yet they were laughing and joking with one another, and willingly smiled at me as I took their picture. There was something about their free and easy manners that attracted me, and I think that perhaps I was a bit jealous of the warmth they openly showed one another. I admired their naturalness.

*   *   *   *

I put a large amount of energy and time into these pictures and was quite pleased with my results. I was amused that my family and friends were so impressed with my street photographs; they talked about my project a great deal. It gave me a sense of accomplishment that up to this point I had only felt in the realm of athletics.

One of the people who heard about my photography was a man who headed up the quarantine station that was located on two islands near my home on Staten Island, a Dr. Doty. The stations on Hoffman and Swinburne islands were where ships that were suspected of carrying people with infectious diseases were held until the threat of imported germs could be eliminated. Sometimes they did this by simply holding the boat, and the immigrants who were considered carriers until the threat of infection passed, and sometimes through deportation of the sickest cases. Dr. Doty approached me one day, quite out of the blue, with a proposition. He felt he had some unique pieces of sterilizing equipment he had designed, and he wanted to have photographs of them. I traveled to the Hoffman and Swinburne islands several times to document Dr. Doty's "special items," and for this I received a payment of $25. This was my first paid employment, and while Dr. Doty was quite pleased with my results, I thought the pictures of the equipment were perhaps the dullest photographs I had ever taken.

The other day, when Mr. Oglesby came, he asked me about the several examples he had with him. I must have gone back to the quarantine stations ten times over the course of ten years to take pictures for the good doctor, and although I liked being paid for my work, I would hate the thought that the pictures of sterilizing ovens and so forth would stand as prime examples of my photographic talents.

I continued to take the photographs for Dr. Doty for two reasons. The first is that I liked the idea of being paid, and the second is that I had become interested in the lives of immigrants. My visits to the stations gave me a chance to see the newest people as they arrived in America. Imagine leaving everything that is familiar—homes, friends, sometimes family, and language—to become American. Their lives here seemed so dismal that sometimes as I took their pictures, I wondered what motivated them to go on living and how they could give me such big and open smiles. Perhaps it was the promise that there would be a better future. After all, the promise of America was that anyone who worked hard could make something of himself.

*   *   *   *

At one point, I had the idea that I might be able to sell some of my pictures of immigrants without becoming involved in a situation, like the one with Dr. Doty, where I was taking pictures that were directed by someone else. So in addition to going to the quarantine stations—where, when I was done with the machines, I could turn my camera to the people who worked or were confined to the islands—I continued to travel to New York to take pictures of working people. As I did this over the course of about a year, a project formed in my mind. It was based on the albums that I had prepared for my friends and family. I would put together an album of selected street photographs, or perhaps a portfolio-type arrangement, and attempt to sell it. I was, after all, thirty years old by this time, a confirmed spinster in my mind, and I felt my life needed some direction, since taking care of a husband and raising children seemed out of the question.

I remember that in 1896 I made a vow to devote myself to my new project. Unlike my first forays, this time I set about covering a large number of neighborhoods, although once again I stayed away from the seediest ones. I also sought to cover a wide array of occupations. And this I did. I photographed immigrants at the Battery who had just arrived from their homelands, cabdrivers, newsboys and newsgirls, messenger boys, hansom cab drivers, ragpickers, street cleaners, postmen, and policemen. I would often become fascinated with one particular type of employment and focus on it for a time, so there were many, many pictures of messengers, postmen, policemen, street sweepers, and news sellers. I even came to know some of these people by name. It was all tremendously exciting to me.

I selected a dozen of the nearly fifty pictures that I took and copyrighted them. I had the Albert Type Company create photogravures, and I mounted the pictures and put them in a portfolio of my own design, calling the entire lot "Street Types." I was very satisfied with the results, and had several sets made. However, I put little effort into marketing them, and therefore realized no money from that venture. I was simply not suited to conducting business. After all, in spite of the fact that I was unmarried, I was still a lady.

After quite a strong start, I abruptly ceased my "Street Types" project and returned to more familiar subjects—my friends, my family, my home, and my social life.

Chapter Seven

Anyone who had the opportunity to look through my entire collection of glass plates would see a woman who was preoccupied for the most part with travel and athletics. My thousands of plates document everywhere I went and all the activities I participated in.

I tell Mr. Oglesby that I had had a larky life, meaning I lived a life devoted to having a good time—one that was seemingly unencumbered by serious problems...until my old age, at least. And for the most part, that was true, but there were some dilemmas that did cause me concern and that preoccupied me, especially as the marriageable age slipped by without an engagement to a gentleman. I tell Mr. Oglesby that I chose not to marry because there was no one who was good enough for me. This is the truth, but it is not the whole truth, and coming to this realization is almost as difficult as coping with the poverty of my later years.

I did make a completely conscious choice not to marry, but before I came to that crossroads, I had been fairly confused as to why I didn't want to have a husband and a home. Papa had made a warm and lovely home for Grandmother, Mama, and me, so I could not understand why I was reluctant to follow that example. I know some people think I did not marry because of my father's treachery, and I also know there was a rumor that I was engaged to a gentleman who accidentally shot himself while cleaning his gun, and therefore my heart was broken. I must say I never disabused anyone of either of those notions. But the latter is a complete falsehood, and the former is only a small, insignificant part of why I did not follow the other girls into marriage.

If someone were forward enough to ask, and I felt I had to give a reason for remaining a spinster, my response would have to be that there was some part of my being that simply did not find men attractive, and I was put off by the idea of having sexual relations with any man. Naturally no one was ever bold enough to ask directly, nor would I ever have felt comfortable giving that sort of answer to anyone. Other girls thought the way I did but went ahead and married anyway. However, I was independent enough to go my own way.

As I lie here now, it seems so obvious and so natural to have never married, just as my being in love and living with my Gertrude was. But it has been far from simple to come to this point in my thinking. And it was, in part, photography that helped guide me to my understanding of myself in this regard.

I did not begin my exploration in order to make a critique of society. In fact I came to the making of a study of relations among women and between men and women without really giving it any conscious thought. People like Mr. Oglesby may think I was trying to explore the meanings of class or the condition of the female versus the male sex, but the truth is that I never said to myself, "I want to make pictures that explore the relationships of the sexes and the place of women in my society." But upon reflection, I think it's true that there are many photographs I have taken that ask and answer questions about these very subjects. I think back to the photograph of Trude and me masked in short skirts, and I realize that picture addresses the deep love I felt for Trude, and it was not simply a sisterly or romantic love, but a sexual attraction as well. The picture of Julia Martin, Mrs. Snively, and me in bed reflects the warmth and comfort I felt around women who were similar to me in the sense that they did not want to be involved with men…especially Julia, who was quite open about her crushes on the other girls.

In a very real sense, I can see that my pictures might express more than I had consciously intended. Look at my "Street Type" photographs. It is clear to me now that a camera can do two separate things: it can be a recording tool or it can be a way of seeing. This difference is not always clear, even to me as the photographer, because there is sometimes a fine line between the two. As I traveled in working-class neighborhoods, I realized that photography was more than a way of making a picture, that it was a way of seeing the world. It was like alchemy in the sense that I could take something ordinary and transform it into something extraordinary. I could take a simple portrait and make it more meaningful by altering the lighting, the pose, the arrangement of objects, by capturing a small gesture...or by more extravagant methods such as the use of costumes and *tableaux vivants*. I see now the deeper meanings that my pictures carried. And I know that with photography, I helped myself to understand and come to some sense of peace with some of what I considered to be the ridiculous manners of my social set, and with the ways in which I was different from other girls.

Quite obviously the photograph of Julia, Julie, and me dressed as men posed a statement about my view of my own sex and the opposite one, but this is a most outrageous example. So many of my pictures seemed to be about an event, but the truth of the matter is that there almost always was a coded message hidden in the picture.

*   *   *   *

In my society, you could always tell a woman's class and identity by how she dressed. When my friends and I appeared in public, we were always very careful with our attire, so as to reflect well on ourselves. I also knew that by wearing a costume, my friends and I could pretend to be something else. In my life, I have worn witch costumes and Spanish dancer outfits, but one disguise that stands out in my mind was that of a nun, from the time Trude and I dressed as nuns at Twilight Rest several years before I met Gertrude. At that time, many of my friends were marrying, and we were all concerned with the proprieties surrounding courtship. A girl and a young man were supposed to behave in a certain way—that is, that both parties would exercise restraint in what we called "making love." Today I think they call it flirting. We all knew what our parents and society in general expected from us. We all knew things did not always happen the way they were supposed to.

For the picture, I remember, Trude and I fashioned nun habits out of some odd pieces of dark fabric and used Pears soap wrappers to make the white border around the face. We left the soap name on the wrappers in order to emphasize the cleanliness and purity that Catholics liked to attribute to the religious sisters. Several other friends who were also in costume for some event wanted to pose for a photograph, and I suppose I could have taken just a portrait of the group, but I always liked to have a little activity in my pictures, so I created a "scene," or *tableau vivant*: The nuns are observing a young maiden, seated in the foreground, who is smiling shyly, yet perhaps a touch too tenderly, at a gentleman soldier. The nuns who watch the scene as chaperones see, but do not really notice, the intimate smiles exchanged by the two chaste young lovers.

Several other friends were in the picture as well, dressed as elderly ladies who see nothing of the exchange. I was particularly satisfied with the solemn faces of the "onlookers," because courtship was considered such a serious business. Yet in truth, it was, in my opinion, rather silly. I do not think my view was very obvious in this picture; perhaps I was too subtle, because no one seemed to realize it was anything other than a straightforward portrait.

As I grew older, I became a little more adept at staging my scenes so that my friends and family—the only people I would show these many very private photographs to—would understand the true significance. I did this of course, with the "no-yes" pictures that I took with Trude and Willie Hopper, and I also did it with a series of photographs I took when I visited Julie Bredt, who had moved to Bethlehem, Pennsylvania. Julie and I had known each other since childhood. She lived in the next house from ours, and her father was quite well-to-do. We were great friends; we shared an interest in music and in photography, although I was more advanced than Julie.

January 15, 1892
Julie Bredt
Bethlehem, Pennsylvania

My dearest Alice,

Well, such is life! I am so sorry that you have not been able to come to visit, as Bethlehem never was so gay. We are having such fun that I will not go away on my winter vacation and will be here until after Lent sometime. Now can you come by the thirteenth of February? Really, Lollie, you must come then—there will be so many social activities, and I have loads of things to tell you. Ahem.

Please come, Lollie, and do not forget to bring your camera. My friends are anxious to pose for you, as I have told them what wonderful pictures you take and how much fun you can be as you direct your little scenes. I have shown several of my closest friends the picture of us with Julia Martin. It is quite startling. Have you heard from Julia, the poor dear? I do not envy her, dispossessed from all that is familiar to her. I must write her a letter.

Lollie, I shall expect you before the thirteenth. Please write soon and advise me of your travel plans. Do not plan to stay less than two weeks. We will have such fun.

Your affectionate and loving friend,
Julie Bredt

*   *   *   *

As Julie had always promised, her friends were willing subjects for my camera. We did an entire series of "Tea Party" photographs, which satirically advanced the notion that all sorts of wild lovemaking went on in secret, even though it was strictly forbidden to unmarried girls (and even unmarried gentlemen). In my set, I showed this by having the ladies and four of the gentlemen standing quite properly, drinking and pouring tea at a table. But in the foreground of several of the pictures, there are two gentlemen who in one photograph are gazing at each other, and who in a second photograph are draped over one another. The two gentlemen are out of sight of the people behind the table—that is, proper society—and therefore the intimacy between the two gentlemen is taking place under the table and out of sight…but not really, since it was in the front of the photograph. It always interested me that we girls and gentlemen were presented with all sorts of societal restrictions that everyone appeared to adhere to in public, but that everyone so widely disregarded in private. As long as the young people weren't flagrant, everyone in our set pretended that we didn't know what was going on. I determined that I wanted to make this paradox a subject of my photographs, and Julie's friends happily went along. I consider these pictures a success, and Julie was quite pleased with them as well.

In my life, I have taken many photographs that deal with this subject: girls smoking, drinking, rejecting suitors, and feigning intimacy with boys are everywhere among my pictures. And Julie and I seemed to take photographs that addressed the subject of courtship every time we were together, whether at her home or at mine. I wonder if the gentlemen in the pictures realized how we were mocking their pretensions of gallantry.

But I was also fascinated by my own attraction to other girls and the pervasiveness of similar attractions among the girls I knew. And while I tended to be satirical when I depicted courtship and relations between ladies and gentlemen, I was that way far less often when photographing the love I saw between two ladies. I remember how after the tennis matches, Nellie Jamieson, dressed in gentlemen's clothing, would lovingly rest her hand on the lap of one of the Roosevelt sisters. Oh, Nellie was so mad about that girl—she wrote for copies of both the pictures I took that day. I would take portraits of my tennis friends or my bicycling friends and see them gently touching or turning away from the camera to gaze into one another's eyes. And there were boys too who had crushes on one another. Lloyd Hyde and Arvid Knudsen loved each other and lived together for decades. I remember one time at their house where Lloyd dressed as minstrel and Arvid dressed as a lady, and they posed together. The pictures were humorous because of the costuming, but the love between them was as serious and as passionate as mine for Gertrude.

When Gertrude and I are pictured together, we are always resting against one another—not in a sensual way, because that was reserved for complete privacy, but in an intimate and romantic way. I never made apologies for my love for Gertrude when we lived together, and I certainly will not begin to make them now.

I also took many, many pictures of Gertrude, and I always cast her in a soft and romantic light, because I felt that best reflected her true person. I remember standing behind her at night as she let down her long hair. After her illness, it had grown back white and wonderfully soft. I would reach for her brush, and I would gently smooth out the waves.

*   *   *   *

I reflect back as I sit here alone in my ghastly wheelchair, waiting for a visit from Mr. Oglesby. He says our talks have helped his project greatly, and we've developed a quaint friendship over the last several months. In my mind, everything seems so clear and well thought out, but it wasn't at the time. I never made a firm decision to make my pictures a study of my feelings and thoughts; that is just what occurred. Not that I was completely unfamiliar with the "philosophers" of photography—like Alfred Stieglitz, who advocated that photography be treated as an art form, a means to express a deeper message or a sharper vision. Everyone who was a true amateur photographer knew about Mr. Stieglitz, but I had an opportunity to become more acquainted with his ideas through my friendship with a friend of Daisy Elliott's.

---

14 April 1891
Daisy Elliott
77 Park Avenue
New York

My dear Alice,

What a surprise I had when I returned home last evening and found at my doorstep an envelope with the pictures of the gymnasium. My, we all look serious, but then as you know, I consider exercise for ladies to be a serious business. Thank you ever so much for leaving the photographs for me; I shall treasure them always.

I do wish I had been home when you left them. I have such an exciting story to tell you. This afternoon, while you were undoubtedly traipsing around the city with your camera, I was dining with Dr. Hyde-Smith, the physician who advocates exercise as a method for ladies to recover and maintain their health. It seems he has a patient, Mrs. De La Guardia, who has traveled here from Mexico with her sister, an unmarried woman, Sara de La Seina. The ladies had been living for a time in Mexico, as the climate was beneficial to the health of Mrs. De La Guardia. Their father is Spanish, but their mother is English; they have been educated in Europe, and their English is excellent. In any case, while in Mexico, Mrs. De La Guardia was stricken with a debilitating illness that is causing her pains in all her extremities, and Dr. Hyde-Smith has recommended that, as part of her treatment, she come to the gymnasium for exercises. I will be meeting with "my patient" tomorrow.

It came out in conversation with Dr. Hyde-Smith that the unmarried sister is quite the photographer, which naturally put me in mind of you, dear Alice. She knows not a soul in New York except the good doctor, and she is naturally somewhat lonely. Perhaps I shall arrange a luncheon for us all—and Carrie, of course, who does not like it when I meet alone with unmarried women. But I do think you and Miss de La Seina will have much in common. Dr. Hyde-Smith says she has been known to traipse about unsavory neighborhoods of London, Paris, and New York with her camera, just like you, old soul. Do let me know which day next week would be convenient for you to lunch with us. I think it would be quite jolly.

I await your response.

Yours affectionately,
Daisy

*   *   *   *

Sara de La Seina was, perhaps, the most exotic-looking woman I have ever known, with thick, wavy black hair the color of midnight and eyes that were so deeply brown, they were almost black as well. Although my friendship with her was intermittent, because she traveled frequently between her homes in Mexico and England with only the briefest of stays in New York, the nature of our relationship was intense. We shared a love of photography, and if I am not mistaken, she and I shared an attraction to women and a lack thereof to men. Mrs. De La Guardia, her sister and traveling companion, seemed distressed at the quantity of time Sara and I spent together, walking the streets with our cameras and talking endlessly about new theories of photography. But I am forever grateful to Daisy for introducing me to Sara, as Sara was the woman who introduced me to the detailed thinking behind the work of Alfred Stieglitz and his group of like-minded photographers. And although I did not agree with everything that Mr. Stieglitz advocated, his theories stimulated my own intellectual interest in the process of photography and the nature of the image itself.

27 April 1892
Sara de La Seina
43 W. Nineteenth Street
New York

My dearest Alice,

What a treat it was last week to dine with you. I have been so lonely here in the United States, as I have only my sister, Rose, for company, and her little boy. I do love my nephew as if he were my own son, but one longs to spend time with someone one's own age. I could not think of a better companion than you, dear Alice. It was difficult to understand how our hours together flew. I do so enjoy discussing the various aspects of photography with you, especially debating the issues that Mr. Stieglitz puts forth in his articles. As you know, he was quite well-known in England, and I believe that soon he will be just as famous in America—not only for his theories, but for his crusty and critical personality.

Alice, my dear, I do hope our meeting marks the beginning of a long and warm friendship for us. It is so difficult for me to find people with whom I can discuss the elements of focus and photographic style for hours on end, but you are such a person. It is refreshing to have a friendship with another lady who is well versed in the elements of photographic style, and you, my dear Alice, are such a wonderful and fascinating companion.

Perhaps we shall have an opportunity to get together again soon. If it is not too forward of me to ask, I would so enjoy visiting your home on the island and meeting your family. Daisy tells me that your mother and grandmother are as fascinating as you, and that your aunt is a wonder. Please do let me know when it might be convenient to meet again.

I am devotedly your friend,
Sara de la Seina

*   *   *   *

As Sara explained it to me, she was familiar with the work of Mr. Stieglitz in Europe since the middle of the 1880s, where he participated in amateur exhibitions and wrote articles for English periodicals. By 1897, however, the year that I met Gertrude, Stieglitz was well established in New York, and his club, the Camera Club of New York, founded a journal that published photographs that were artistic, rather than being documentary in style. I knew of Mr. Stieglitz from his previous role as an editor of the *American Amateur Photographer*, a journal I read religiously throughout the early 1890s. The magazine was always a mine of technical material on photography and processing, but when Mr. Stieglitz took over as coeditor, he introduced new sections devoted to the artistic aspects of photography. I think these articles were on some level a driving force behind my idea for "Street Types."

Sara was a member of the New York Camera Club, and therefore she had a collection of both the *American Amateur Photographer* and *Camera Notes*, the journal that was published by the New York Camera Club. We spent countless hours reviewing the individual pictures in both these periodicals and discussing the ideas behind them. The main thought behind the work in *Camera Notes* was that photography was not simply a mechanical science that recorded fact; it was, in its own right, an art form—as fine an art form as sculpture or painting. I felt very strongly that Mr. Stieglitz was right about this. Sara and I were both appalled by the way in which the Kodak camera had altered the nature of photography. Everywhere I went, it seemed that people were carrying those gadgets and pushing the button, taking pictures without regard to composition and lighting. Snap, snap, snap—without a thought in the world, as if photography were a sport, like hunting or trap shooting. Sara and I both knew that a good photograph requires at least a minimum of thought. There were a few topics, however, on which Sara and I disagreed. While Sara was enamored with fuzzy or soft focus to create a painterly effect, I preferred to stick with the style of sharp focus, feeling that while photography was certainly an art form, photography and painting were two different arts that should not be blended.

Sara considered herself a pictorialist; she concentrated her efforts on landscapes, studies of individuals, and neighborhood scenes. One area in which we were in ready agreement was the necessity of seeking out exotic locations for our photographs; ideal subject matter could always be found close at hand—at home even, in my case. While my pictures were sharply focused so that each and every object was clear to the eye, Sara's images were simply composed and free of detail. In this way, she sought to copy the essence of paintings. Whereas I often sought to transcribe reality, Sara's pictures were taken with an eye to beautifying and glorifying the scene. She thought this helped communicate her thoughts and feelings. I strongly disagreed. I believe my feelings could readily be made clear with sharply focused pictures. But I did see her point, and her photographs were beautiful—one might even say romantic.

I did love Sara's portraiture. Her European education had included classes in painting and drawing, and she was able to translate some of that skill to photographic portraits. Sara introduced me to the work of Gertrude Kasebier, who was considered the preeminent pictorial portraitist and had her own studio in New York City, where she took portraits of many well-known figures in government. She always kept her images simple, and often the focus was soft. The results were beautiful, especially her painterly portraits of women and mothers with their children. I tried to copy her work in this area with limited success. The closest I came were the portraits I made of Julie Bredt and myself dressed in our best clothes on the piazza. They were in fact beautiful portraits, but they did not match the painterly quality of the photographs of Mrs. Kasebier or of my friend Sara. As for my many other portraits, they tended to be quite straightforward and sharply focused, except for my pictures of Gertrude, which were always softly lit and focused and exceptionally warm and beautiful. Perhaps, unlike Sara, I could only take a romantic portrait when I felt the romance in my soul. While I was jealous of Sara's portrait-taking ability, I never felt I was lacking when it came to romantic vision. My romantic vision came through as clearly as Sara's. I only had to look at my beloved Gertrude to achieve that. When I photographed my Gertrude, I tried to copy the style of Mrs. Kasebier…and I did so, I would add, with great success.

Over the course of seven or eight years, Sara and her sister traveled to New York for various treatments, and these visits gave us a chance to examine one another's work and discuss new ideas. Eventually we lost touch. Rose was often so sick that she could no longer leave the house, and eventually she and Sara settled permanently in Mexico. I feel sad having lost the friendship of this very interesting woman and able photographer.

12 March 1899
Sara de la Seina
Pueblo, Mexico

My dearest Alice,

I do apologize from the very bottom of my heart for not writing you sooner. You must think I ought to be ashamed of myself, and certainly my neglect of you must seem rude, but I have had so much trouble since last time I was in New York and saw you that I am sure you will forgive me.

The winter has been very trying to us all, but my sister's baby has suffered the most…so much so that we are compelled to remain in Mexico, where the climate is better for my nephew and sister. We left for Mexico quite suddenly at the end of January, and I was sorely disappointed, as I had hoped to see you and your lovely friend Gertrude before my departure. It is a great disappointment to me that I have not had the pleasure of seeing you for some time, but these few lines will have to say my good-bye for a good long time. Rose is to travel to Mexico City to consult a doctor, and I shall go with her. It is impossible to tell how long we shall be forced to remain there.

As our steamer sailed out of New York, I did look for your house, in spite of the fact that I was feeling ill myself—perhaps it was the heartbreak of my sudden departure and not seasickness, as the ship's doctor thought. It was so difficult for me to leave, and I do hope we can continue our friendship by mail. I am enclosing several of my prints—some lovely photographs of you and Miss Tate; I think that they are quite beautiful, but then you are two beautiful ladies.

Until we meet again, believe me, dear Alice, I remain your devoted and loving friend.

Sara de la Seina

Chapter Eight

Mr. Oglesby is here this afternoon, asking me about my photographs of immigrants. What did I have in mind? Why did I choose this subject? Was there an "ulterior reason" for undertaking the project, as he calls it? Of course I began by taking pictures for Dr. Doty on the quarantine station. I became curious as to what happened to these poor homeless souls when they left isolation, so I followed them to the Battery, where they were dropped off by ship, and then I followed them to the neighborhoods, where they settled. Sara and I had spoken several times of Jacob Riis, a gentleman who made a life's work of photographing immigrants in order to show their plight in the New World, so I was simply curious. The 1890s saw such a huge wave of immigration. It was all over the newspapers, and people in government were constantly warning that our race was becoming polluted by this influx of foreigners with strange customs and loose lifestyles.

12 April 1896
Alice Austen
2 Pennsylvania Avenue
Rosebank

Dear Sara,

I have just returned from a day of taking pictures in the city, and rather than feeling exhausted from my travails, I feel exhilarated. It is as though the ghetto streets that breathe with life have breathed new life into my soul. There is no equal to the life of the city streets. Amid the rank and dark tenements, I heard both squeals of delight and shouts of anger. Everything is done in public—fighting and making love and playing with friends and shopping for food. No emotion is ever hidden in the ghettos of the East Side of New York. Business is conducted in small shops, but also in the gutter. Love is made in the alleyways. And children play along the filthy side streets. Older children hawk newspapers and shoelaces or run errands for shopkeepers. I saw some raggedy old soul exchange his possessions for money with a Jew while women on the corner haggled over prices for bread and eggs. Their lives seemed so miserable, yet they seemed so full of life; it is hard to reconcile. Every moment seems a struggle, and still they laugh and smile when I ask them to pose for my camera.

It is easy to see how these immigrant lives could become a plague on our race. In the last several years, these wretched people have flooded our shores, bringing their diseases and their filth and their foreign customs to our city. How their population seems to grow daily and the noise and the disorder of their lives spreads out from their own little neighborhoods. Woe to the Anglo-Saxon race and to America if these people should take over these United States. These immigrants are fascinating to watch and to photograph, and something about their lives is thrilling to me, but America must beware, lest we be overtaken by them.

Dearest Sara, whenever shall you return to New York? I do miss our talks and our exchanges of ideas—your view of photography is so different from mine, and the conversations we have stimulate me so. The recollection of our last talk about Mr. Riis and his nighttime forays in immigrant neighborhoods with Police Commissioner Roosevelt encouraged me to take my camera to the East Side today, but I fear if we do not meet face-to-face sometime soon, all my enthusiasms will fade to nothingness.

Please send my best to your sister and your handsome little nephew. I do hope that Rose is feeling better and that you will be able to return to New York when the weather is more suitable. Daisy tells me that she misses her favorite "patient."

I am, as always, your affectionate and devoted friend,
Alice

*   *   *   *

What can I tell Mr. Oglesby? I tell him the truth: that I was simply curious. I wasn't like Mr. Riis, who photographed new immigrants struggling under harsh conditions. I was not trying to influence anyone with my pictures. Sara and I had discussed the fact that Mr. Riis hoped to improve the living conditions of the poor with his photographs, but I had no such interest. Certainly the conditions in which they lived were abysmal, but that was their own doing—they brought their slovenly customs with them from the Old World, and if their lives were too raggedy and dirty for them, then they would have to change them themselves. It was not the government's place. America offered more opportunity than any other country in the world, and it was up to those new immigrants to use the opportunities they were offered.

The United States was growing by leaps and bounds in those days. Every day it seemed there was a new invention that made life easier and a new factory opening up offering jobs to the immigrants who came here with few to no skills. America was the land of opportunity, and I was always proud of my country. I was especially proud of the United States' role in the spring of 1898, during the Spanish American War.

---

2 January 1899
Alice Austen
2 Pennsylvania Avenue
Rosebank, Staten Island

Sara dear,

My dear Sara, let me begin by wishing you and your sister and her whole family best wishes for a happy New Year. I cannot believe, somehow, that this is the end of the nineteenth century, and what a busy century it has been—from the infant years of this new republic through the great conflict between the states and finally to glorious victory in the Spanish American War. I have enclosed several prints I made during the many parades that memorialized the United States' latest victory. You know how I love a good parade. Remember my countless pictures of the Columbus Naval Parades in 1892 and 1893 and of the Grant Parade on the president's birthday that same year?

I must admit, I have been positively swept up by the patriotic fervor that seems to have gripped the nation in the wake of our country's decisive triumphs. Some people, especially the financiers with interests in Cuban sugar plantations, were dreadfully opposed to becoming involved in a war against Spain, because it threatened the American bankers' investments, but how could America stand idly by as our battleship the *Maine* was mined? How could we stand by while a hundred thousand Cubans were mercilessly killed by Spanish repression? The papers were filled daily with atrocities committed by the Spanish government. I know that as a nation, the United States is and should be proud of its involvement in this "splendid little war." It seems as though the whole country has been brought together by this experience; North and South, East and West, native and immigrant alike—all can take pride in the accomplishments of Commodore Dewey's victory in Manila Bay in the Philippines and our other naval victories in Cuba. We can be especially proud of the feats of Theodore Roosevelt and his Rough Riders at San Juan Hill. It is all so glorious and spectacular.

And now that the war has been won, America has its own little empire with Puerto Rico and the Philippines, and our relationship with Cuba is better than it was under the Spanish. Those naysaying financiers were wrong in their hesitation; indeed they have benefited from America's victory.

One wonders, dear Sara, what the next century will bring. Without a doubt, the United States will lead the way with new inventions and new industries, and we will continue to grow and be powerful. The world will look to the United States as a leader. I am, I know, a great optimist, but I feel that I am correct.

Well, Sara, once again wishing you and yours a wonderful New Year.

I am forever your devoted friend,
Alice

*   *   *   *

I shall talk to Mr. Oglesby about my belief in the greatness of America, and I shall talk to him about my photographs in and about New York City…but what shall I say about Gertrude? Can I tell the whole story? I was raised to believe there were certain things a lady should not discuss, and even though I am living in this poorhouse, I am still very much a lady.

Chapter Nine

March 4, 1898
Alice Austen
Rosebank, Staten Island

Dearest Gertrude,

I have just come from my little closet darkroom, and late as it is, I knew I could not sleep unless I wrote to you first, my darling. I have developed the plates I made of your beautiful visage, and tonight I printed several of the photographs. As I touched your face on the paper, I longed to touch your own beautiful skin. I longed even for a touch of your fingertips. I do not know how I can live these days apart from you. In the short time that we have known each other, you have come to occupy a large space in my heart, and when you are gone from me, my heart feels empty and hollow.

As you saw for yourself on this most recent visit, Mama is feeling poorly and seems to feel worse by the day. I do not think I shall leave home this summer, as Mama needs constant care that I feel only I can give. Perhaps, dear Gertrude, you would be willing to spend part of the summer here with me on the island? I have begun to worry about the day that Mama will no longer be with me, occupying the bed beside me in our beautiful, light bedroom. I shall feel very lonely, but in this difficult time, I am reassured by your presence in my life. You are my salvation. You are so kind and gentle and good, dearest angel.

Before we met, dear Gertrude, I could never truly believe that one woman could love another woman as I love you. I know that I could never love any man enough to spend the rest of my life with him. Ah, but you, dearest one...I could certainly be with you every waking hour for eternity and even longer, if such a thing exists. I love your whole being. I love your voice, your eyes, your lips, and your delicate hands, with which you caress me. I long to hold you in my arms, angel of mine, and to touch your warm and loving breasts, to hear our hearts beat as one. Our hours alone are precious jewels and are worth more than gold.

When shall we see each other again? Every moment apart seems to be a lifetime; every day is an eternity. You are my love and my life; you are the center of my universe. You are the sun and the moon and the stars. I shall love you always and forever and a day, darling.

With total love and devotion,
Alice

October 1900
Alice Austen
Rosebank, Staten Island

Dearest Julia,

As my dear friend, Miss Tate, wrote you recently, Mama has passed on. I have neglected to write you myself because of my grief. I have lost so many people dear to me in recent years—Papa, Grandmother, and Uncle Oswald. It makes one realize how short life is and how long eternity will be. I shall never see, nor speak to these loved ones again, and that is hard for me to realize, because they were so important to my life and were and still are so dear to my heart.

Mama's death is extremely difficult for me. I would have totally lost my mind, were it not for the loving presence of my dear Gertrude, who is my pillar of support in trying times. I do think that losing one's mother is the hardest loss of all. Never again will I feel the warmth of her maternal touch or hear the softness of her loving voice. There will never again be motherly words of warm comfort in the difficult times. Mama was ever so brave, and she protected me from harm and torment, especially that caused by my father's abandonment. I have been blessed with a loving mother, and that is more than one could ask for. Her life was long, and if not a happy one, then at least a peaceful one once she returned home to Clear Comfort. I shall miss her terribly.

I have not much else to say, as I have been so involved in my mourning. Thank you so much for your kind words of comfort. They mean so much to me, especially from you, dear Julia, so far away in California. I hope this letter finds you in better health. Please write again soon; I enjoy hearing about your adventures on the "frontier." Miss Tate sends her regards.

With love and affection,
Alice

*   *   *   *

I had loved my mother so deeply, and when she was gone, I experienced a terrible emptiness. Gertrude, of course, saved me from the isolation of having no family, but in truth I had no family left. Especially after Uncle Pete died, my family world such as it was spun apart, and I was left virtually orphaned. Even at the age of thirty-four, which is how old I was when Mama died, I felt orphaned. And now I am here isolated and alone in this poorhouse.

*   *   *   *

Mr. Oglesby stopped by today to tell me the good news, as he calls it, that my photographs are to be published in *Life* magazine and in *Holiday*. He assures me that all the proceeds from the sale of my pictures will go to me, which I feel is good news. Perhaps now I will escape this wretched poverty and move to a more suitable home. However, I am nervous about the publication of my pictures—many of them were meant to be seen by only a few select people. I am afraid that some of the pictures that I have taken will reveal more about me and my friends than I want anyone to know.

I am especially worried someone might be able to deduce that Gertrude and I are something more than friends. I have never discussed this openly with anyone. I am sure that most of my close friends realize the nature of the relationship, but we never talk about it. I have always been alone in my feelings. As a young lady, I envied girls who fell in love with boys. They were able to share every moment of their courtships and the lovely feelings that come with falling in and being in love. But for women like myself, I know that rule is "don't talk." What am I to do when asked about my life with Gertrude? I could never divulge the truth, no matter how beautiful it has been. I wish there were someone I could ask, but even if Mama were alive...or Papa, or Grandmother, or even Aunt Minn...I could never ask them. Sometimes I feel truly alone in this world.

Fortunately for me, Gertrude had moved into Clear Comfort after Aunt Minn died in 1917 so that I was not alone. But I was happier about being with Gertrude in our own home than I was about no longer feeling lonely. I loved Gertrude with all of my soul and my heart. And we were a family. We went through the bad times together and enjoyed the good times. In 1909 Gertrude and I took a long summer trip to Europe, touring Germany, Switzerland, and the Netherlands. We traveled to Paris together and to London, and these were some of our best times. I think you know you love someone when you are able to have a wonderful time alone together, and Gertrude and I certainly did.

Mr. Oglesby wants to hear all about my larky life, but I cannot tell all. Perhaps I would do well to stick to talking about my photographs of the quarantine station or my "Street Types" or my photographs of parades. I took countless pictures of parades.

I do not know what to do. So many of my pictures were not meant for general circulation. What will people think of Julie, Julia, and me dressed as men...and that umbrella that Julia is holding? I certainly shan't address that. I must keep silent on many things, but above all I must keep silent about my relationship with my beloved Gertrude. There is a part of me that wants to tell everything, a part that wants to profess my undying love for my angel Gertrude. I love her so deeply. But I can say nothing. In truth it is no one's business, but I am so proud of the love I feel that sometimes I am almost bursting. My body is crippled, but when I think of Gertrude, my mind dances a jig, and I feel strong in my heart.

But still, I cannot announce my feelings to the world. My love for Gertrude is so pure, yet I know there are those who find that kind of love sick and disgusting and who would heap scorn on Gertrude and me, were they to know the truth about our relationship. This I could not bear. I am a lady, and I must keep up appearances.

Chapter Ten

Yesterday morning I woke up at seven as usual, and the nurse escorted me to the bathroom for a sponge bath and to take care of necessities. She helped me put on one of my two dresses and sat me in my wheelchair. I was expecting a visit from Gertrude and was looking forward to embracing her and stroking her pale, soft cheeks. But to my surprise, not only did Gertrude arrive at nine—earlier than usual—but Mr. Oglesby and a small entourage of assistants walked in. They packed my meager possessions and transported me via automobile to this lovely, sunny private home.

I am now settled in a small room of my own on the ground floor. It is such an unexpected and blessed relief to no longer be in the poorhouse. I am no longer in that place where I am confronted by my own wretched poverty. Of course my surroundings are not as grand as my home was, but it is comfortable, and I am treated with the respect I was used to when I was younger. Mr. Oglesby and Gertrude keep telling me that next week there will be a day of the big celebration honoring me. Magazines have published my photographs. I have become famous, I am told.

Soon I shall return to Clear Comfort for a visit, and I am quite excited at the prospect. But I have been warned that my home is a mere shadow of its former self. The immigrants who bought my home for pennies on the dollar have allowed it to fall to rack and ruin. No matter. I can't wait to see the terrace, to sit on the piazza, and to see the parlor. How I have dreamed of this day: a last chance to see my home, my Clear Comfort.

*   *   *   *

No words could have prepared me for the condition of my beautiful home. The whole place was a shambles. The outside was unpainted; the shutters were askew. Inside it reminded me of the tenements from the East Side of New York, with people having spread their belongings and their garbage all over the place without regard for my home's great history. The gardens and the terrace were a virtual jungle. As I sat helpless in my wheelchair, I cried at the sight. They tell me they are raising money to buy my home back and to restore it, but as far as I can see, Clear Comfort is past redemption. My home, my beautiful home, is no more. It is a dreadful ghost that shows no reflection of its former glory. Who could have believed that it once housed the finest of ladies and gentlemen?

And Gertrude and I were both ladies. In spite of the fact that neither of us married and raised a family, we were ladies by virtue of the exemplary lives we led. We were honorable, and we were never loud or showy. We knew how to keep what was private to ourselves and our inner circle. Now I am being asked questions about my life, and I am forced to decide if I should become like my home—a shadow of my former self. Can I be the lady who reveals the most private details of her life? Can I be the one who declares out loud that I have loved, and am still in love with, another woman? And should I? My whole life, I have maintained appearances—this is what separated my behavior from that of the working girls who flirted with abandon in the streets before everyone's eyes. I do not think I can violate that code of behavior now, even though I am old and needy. I may be poor, but I am still a lady.

*   *   *   *

It is a beautiful Sunday. Gertrude has been to see me with Mr. Oglesby. It's been about six months since I first met Mr. Oglesby, and I'm grateful for his visits, because they made me reflect on my life and appreciate all I've experienced. We talked about the past—my larky life. Those were the days when I could engage in all manner of athletics, when I could sing and dance. Those were the days that Gertrude and I dined at the finest restaurants and went to the opera and the theater, when we traveled to London and Paris, and when we shopped on the Rue St. Honoré for handmade gloves and custom-made hats. It was a time before the wars and before the crash of the stock market. It was a time when a lady could be a lady. I know those days are gone now, but still I long for their return—the days when my Gertrude and I could stroll down the street arm in arm and when we could return home together and hold each other in a loving embrace. There are no private moments for love now. And all that is left of them is the yearning for their return.

Mr. Oglesby asks about these things, and I tell him all about the games I played, the cycling I did, and the music that I enjoyed. I talk to him about my graceful home and Papa, Grandmother, and Mama. I tell him about the fun that I had with Uncle Oswald, Aunt Minn, and Uncle Pete. I mention canal boat trips, summering in the mountains, and visits to Europe and to the Chicago World's Fair. He shows me pictures of my friends joking before the camera, and I tell him that there is no other meaning to these games than the fun of them. And in part, that is true.

But there is more, and I long to tell him that we staged these *tableaux vivants* for a reason, that we made up these jokes to express what we were really feeling. But I cannot tell him, and I will not tell him. I cannot say that the lovely romantic pictures I took of Gertrude say what I really feel. I cannot tell him that I loved my Gertrude more than life itself, and that my world would feel totally empty without her. As I grow older, I become more certain this is a story I will take to my grave. Gertrude will know, and I shall know, but no one else will. We are ladies, and our love is private. We shall go to our graves knowing that we loved and cared about one another in a way that was greater than the greatest love on earth, but no one else will know.

This is a lovely porch, and the breeze feels so gentle on my face—like Gertrude's tender and delicate hand caressing my cheek. I need to close my eyes for just a moment and savor that memory.

Postscript

On June 26, 1952, as Miss Alice Austen sat on the porch, she closed her eyes and drifted off to sleep. She died at 3:10 in the afternoon without ever waking, and she never told her story.

1499144

Made in the USA